Johnnie

By

Iain R. Sykes

Copyright © 2018 Iain R. Sykes

ISBN: 978-0-244-68509-6

All rights reserved, including the right to reproduce this book, or portions thereof in any form. No part of this text may be reproduced, transmitted, downloaded, decompiled, reverse engineered, or stored, in any form or introduced into any information storage and retrieval system, in any form or by any means, whether electronic or mechanical without the express written permission of the author.

PublishNation
www.publishnation.co.uk

Dedication

To the wonderful, unique people of the Isle of Lewis.

Chapter 1

Calum thought to die at only 17 years of age was dreadfully sad.

As the dark, peaty water of the Willow Glen river swirled round him, Calum's lungs felt as if they were bursting. He needed to draw breath, but he knew he would only take in water. His arms were flailing, trying to raise his head above the water, but he was in deep trouble. Like the river, his mind was a maelstrom. He hoped against hope he would come out of this alive.

Suddenly, he sensed someone else was in the water near him. He was grabbed by strong arms and pulled against the current. Very soon, he was heaved out of the water and dragged, sopping wet, on to the path beside the river on his back. Ecstatic to see the light again, the boy took in a huge, welcome breath. Exhaling loudly, Calum gave a mighty cough and spluttered out copious amounts of water. He could see a man's figure above him and felt someone pushing violently on his chest, causing him to bring up even more water. He was turned on his front and further air and water were squeezed out. After a minute or so of this treatment, the exhausted boy lay breathing heavily. He opened his eyes. It felt great to be alive.

Raising his head, he turned his right shoulder and vomited violently. This didn't last long, however, and soon Calum was back breathing rapidly but reasonably normally again. In the pale autumn sun, he looked up to see the man who had saved him, leaning over him together with an old man with a wrinkled face, also bent over intently.

"You ok?" asked the boy's saviour with a worried frown. Calum nodded in groggy agreement.

"Thank God for that!" exclaimed the older man standing beside him, "Sit over on that bench for a couple of minutes to get your breath back."

So with some help, he heaved himself up and went over to the wooden bench-seat, completely sodden and bedraggled. By now a crowd of half a dozen had formed.

"It's the Sutcliffe lad from Perceval Rd," the old man said. "Know the family well." Calum recognised him as old Kenny Morrison, a retired Harris Tweed mill-worker in his seventies. "Tell you what, Calum, you're lucky this brave man here was passing. Saved your life, he did! I saw you were in trouble, but I'm too rickety and decrepit to help. Heavens, I was a hell of a swimmer when I was young. I'd have dragged you out in ten seconds flat in those days," he boasted.

At this, another old man in the crowd gave Kenny a disbelieving and disparaging look. The hero of the day was sitting, wringing wet, beside the young lad on the bench-seat. As Calum turned to thank him, he had his first real look at the drenched stranger. He appeared about 30 years old, very tall and sparely built. A bit of a bean-pole. His face was distinctive too, with a large forehead and long chin. He had a very noticeable pallor, almost anaemic, beneath a head of thin, straggly, blond hair. He was wearing a blue anorak, denim shirt and blue jeans.

"Come on, young lad," ordered Kenny, putting his hand under Calum's arm, "and we'll get you home. "Looking at the thin man, he motioned to him. "You too. Catriona'll soon get you dried out and make you a nice cup of tea." He winked "…..or maybe a wee dram to warm you up."

The crowd dispersed as the three of them walked the three hundred yards to where Calum lived, the dripping-wet stranger wheeling his bicycle along beside him. Calum walked in first through the back door into the kitchen with the other two following, leaving a wet wake behind them like a snail trail. Leaving his bike outside, the blond man carried his backpack, which was dry, since he had flung it off before he jumped in the river. Catriona, Calum's mother, a jolly, plump woman of 41, looked them both up and down, hands on hips, with an aghast and slightly deprecating expression.

"What the blazes happened to you lot?" Slumping down in a wooden kitchen chair, Kenny relayed the story in a histrionic way, relishing the theatricality of it all. How her son had been running full pelt along the bank when he slipped and skidded into the river. The river isn't usually deep but after a few weeks of very wet autumn weather, the water was right up to the banks and very fast moving. And how this brave young man had jumped in and saved the day. Thanking the stranger profusely, Catriona asked him his name.

"Johnnie," he replied.

Calum suddenly realised that in all the excitement, he hadn't asked him this himself. Also, the stranger hadn't spoken a word since asking how Calum was after he had resuscitated him.

"I'll get you both some dry clothes. Would you like a cup of tea afterwards, Johnnie?" asked Catriona. When he looked a bit reticent, "….or maybe a hot orange drink?"

"That would be nice, thanks."

"Kenny?"

Lowering his head and flashing a sly look, "Eh… mm… well, maybe something a wee bit stronger, Catriona?" obviously feeling his florid story-telling entitled him to a more generous reward than tea. She smiled conspiratorially and went to the cupboard to fetch a glass and bottle of whisky.

In a matter of ten minutes, Johnnie and Calum had both dried off with a towel. The boy had a clean pair of blue jeans and an open-necked plaid shirt. Johnnie was in a pair of borrowed striped pyjamas and dressing-gown. After a few more minutes of joining up the loose ends of the afternoon's dramatic events, Kenny squinted his sharp blue eyes over his spectacles at Johnnie.

"Don't say a lot, do you? Where you from?"

"Norway."

"Oh aye," intoned Kenny after a small sip of his Glenmorangie, savouring the smoky, amber liquor like a connoisseur. As a pensioner, he normally couldn't afford a malt whisky like Glenmorangie. "I thought you looked very Scandinavian. A bit peely-wally. I suppose you don't get the chance to do much sunbathing in the fjords, do you?"

Ignoring the lame joke, Johnnie sat down at the kitchen table opposite him, explaining he was here on holiday for a few weeks. Then he was looking for a job, maybe as a handyman since he was good at mending and making things.

"Where you staying?"

"I was just about to arrange bed and breakfast after cycling through Willow Glen." It was hard to place his accent, which was not very pronounced anyway. It didn't sound Norwegian to Calum but then again, what did he know, a seventeen-year-old school-kid from a small, windswept Hebridean island off the North West coast of Scotland? If it wasn't Norwegian, no-one could place exactly where it did come from. And anyway, who was about to argue with the man who had just saved the lucky lad's life?

"Well, you're welcome to stay here. It's the least we can do," Calum's mother offered with a grateful smile. "We've got plenty of space since…eh…recently. I'll put you in the back bedroom."

"She makes great bacon and eggs, too," enthused Kenny. "Great with marags. Stornoway black puddings to you, Johnnie. Local delicacy. Anyway, it's about time I was off," he said rising from the chair with a surprising sprightliness belying his age. Not quite so rickety and decrepit as all that, then. "Thanks for the Glenmorangie, Catriona."

When Kenny had gone, the stranger explained he'd had a long journey that day and would they mind if he had a nap. As it turned out, he didn't come out of his room until the following morning.

Perhaps it's time to explain a bit about the people and the island they lived on. This strange tale commences in autumn of 1963. Calum Sutcliffe was a schoolboy of seventeen, born and bred in Stornoway, the only town on the Isle of Lewis, (the rest are villages), the largest and most northerly island in a slightly crescent-shaped archipelago of wind-swept islands in the Outer Hebrides. Or The Western Isles to give it its alternative name. Off the North West coast of Scotland, Lewis was then four and a half hours from the mainland by the steamship, Loch Seaforth, from Kyle of Lochalsh on the Scottish mainland, or twenty-five minutes by air from Inverness. When you have crossed The Minch, the storm-tossed, unpredictable stretch of water in between, you reach this craggy, peaty, rocky outpost, known in the local Gaelic as Eilean Fraoich (Froh-eech), Heather Island. The southern part of the island is called Harris and the whole island is about 60 miles long with a population of around 25,000 in 1963. Stornoway, the seaport and capital of the island represented about 6,000 of that total.

Although Calum is a good old Highland name, short for Malcolm, there was only one Sutcliffe family on the island. Calum's father, Harry, was a Yorkshireman posted during the Second World War to the RAF radar base near Stornoway in 1943 where he met a local girl, Catherine Macleod, (Catriona in Gaelic, which is pronounced with the emphasis on the letter "i", not the "o" as most English speakers think) at a dance and they married in 1945. Calum's father, came from Batley in the industrialised part of Yorkshire, but his weekend hobby had been hill-walking in the Yorkshire Dales before the war. As a result, he loved the island, its rugged terrain and its equally rugged people, so they stayed on after the war.

Calum was born in 1946. They lived in a pebble-dashed, four-bedroom, detached house with a 2 acre field at the back in Perceval Road, a 300-yard long street right on the edge of town. Calum attended the Nicholson Institute in Stornoway, the largest school on the island. He was a very articulate, academic boy, at the top of his class and destined for university. Tall for his age with straight, mousey-blond hair and all the brash confidence of youth, Calum's favourite sport was football, playing inside-right for the best of the local junior teams, United Rovers. He had a sister, Kathy, who was seven years younger. Kathy had been born with a severe hearing problem and lived in Edinburgh where she went to Donaldson's School for the Deaf, a special school for children who are hard of hearing. During term-time, she stayed in a Church of Scotland home for girls. However, she came home to Stornoway for all the major holidays like Easter, Christmas and Summer.

Out of the blue, the family's lives were shattered in January that year, when Harry was killed in a road crash. Going too fast, a large lorry skidded on an icy corner and careered into his car. Harry didn't stand a chance. It was heart-breaking for the whole family. They were all still traumatised, with nightmares and insomnia an on-going problem. Harry had good life insurance and Catriona got substantial compensation from the lorry driver's insurers, so they had no money worries at all. However, they would all have traded all that and more to have Harry back.

The following morning, Johnnie emerged from his room at about 8 o'clock. Calum was sitting at the kitchen table watching his mother making bacon and eggs. He loved to see his mother cooking. As if life was normal again. It made him feel safe. She used to hum a tune quietly as she worked, but not so much these days since Harry's death. That was too much to expect. This morning, however, she was in a jolly mood.

"Good morning, Johnnie Quiet, how are you today?" she said with a mischievous smile.

"Pardon?" he asked with a frown.

She chuckled loudly. "The postman's just told me that the story of what happened yesterday has spread. Kenny's been telling all his pals the tale, suitably embellished no doubt. He's nicknamed you

Johnnie Quiet - or Samhach in Gaelic (<u>sah</u>-vach). Everyone likes it and it's likely to stick."

Johnnie revealed a slight smile. It obviously pleased him. Putting some bread in the toaster, Catriona explained that nicknames are a special thing in Lewis.

"About twenty five surnames cover ninety per cent of the population. My mother was a Macleod from the West Side of Lewis. but she didn't need to change her name when she married my father Alec. He was also a Macleod but from Bayble in the Point area on the East side. So.... to cut a long story short" she went on animatedly, "if someone asks "Do you know John Macleod (or Calum Macdonald or Donald Morrison)?" you'd probably have to say "Which John Macleod?" But if nearly everyone's got a nickname, it's an awful lot easier. Some of the nicknames are quite ingenious. It's actually become an art," she chuckled. "The local representative of the RSPCA....". Seeing Johnnie's querulous expression she expanded, "....The Royal Society for the Prevention of Cruelty to Animals. Well, <u>his</u> nickname's "Cruelty." Everyone knows him as that. So if you mention Cruelty's son, I know exactly who you mean."

Calum warmed to the story. "All the teachers have one too. Mr. Macphail, the Geography teacher, he's called "faoileag," (<u>fuh</u>-lag) Gaelic for seagull, because he's hen-toed and flaps his arms when he walks."

Johnnie grinned as Calum strutted about hen-toed with his arms flapping in imitation.

"Calum!" said his mother sharply with a disapproving look, but secretly trying to smother an incipient smile, "don't be so disrespectful. He's a good teacher."

"What about the Sutcliffes?" asked Johnnie.

"We don't have one. Because the name's unique in Lewis, we don't need one," she replied with a shrug. "Anyway….. let's get our priorities right first. Bacon and eggs all round?"

"Sorry, I'm a vegetarian."

They raised their eyebrows and looked quizzically at him. Vegetarianism was unusual in those days. So they were all surprised and intrigued.

"I'll make you a salad, then. Moral or health reasons?"

"Health. I only drink fruit-juice and water, but not out of the tap. I'd prefer to drink the rain-water from that water barrel at the back of the house if it's ok with you." They all looked at him with confused expressions.

"Tap water's full of poisons," he explained with a look of mild distaste.

He's a rum one all right, Johnnie Quiet, Calum thought, but kept it to myself.

Later in the day, everyone sat round the fire playing board games and discussing different subjects. It was obvious Johnnie was highly intelligent and very well-read. It had been a long time since they'd all had such fun and entertaining company since Harry died. Calum and his mother actually joked and laughed a few times. Laughter wasn't a common event recently in this house. Because Catriona could see that this strange and mysterious man was a good influence on Calum, she found herself asking him to stay on for a few weeks. He'd have his own room and could pay for his keep by doing a few odd jobs. Johnnie accepted without any persuasion.

Everyone wanted to know more about Johnnie's background but he wasn't very expansive about it. It was obvious he didn't want to discuss it in much detail, so the family backed off. His new nickname was well-earned.

Over the next few weeks, Johnnie started to become an integral part of the family. He was a great handyman and had a calming effect on Calum and his mother. They began to sleep better and the nightmares became less common. Johnnie was a bit of a polymath and discussed all sorts of things with them - philosophy, history, science and much else besides. He was a consummate teacher and had a way of making it all seem interesting. His manner was naturally polite but firm, in a quiet, unostentatious way. If he had strong emotions, he never showed them. Phlegmatic, that's the word.

Yet, he was also a truly enigmatic figure. An eccentric. Even on fairly overcast days he often wore sunglasses, saying his eyes were very sensitive. He ate very sparingly, but drank plenty of rainwater from the rain-barrel at the back of the house. Laconic and dignified, he chose his words as if they were precious jewels. However, if asked for his opinion he would usually give it, in a very confident, measured and philosophical way – and usually after thinking for a second first. He had a huge fund of wise quotations which he often used to make his point. What's more, he had an eidetic, photographic memory and could remember long screeds of text from books to quote from. Sometimes, he ascribed them to the originator. Other times, he didn't bother. Apart from some use of irony, he didn't seem to have much of a sense of humour, though. Actually, that's a bit unfair. It was almost as if what he had to say was too serious to crack jokes about it. You could imagine him in the old Roman senate with Cicero and Cato. Full of gravitas and dignitas. However, unlike them, Johnnie wasn't self-important or arrogant. Charisma without ostentation.

However, when there were visitors from outside the family, he avoided getting involved in the conversation as much as possible. Although he didn't slink away, he would often quietly excuse himself suddenly finding a job that needed doing. "I'll just carry on with mending that chair in the kitchen," he might say. The initial frisson of curiosity from the neighbours after the rescue had settled down to a degree, but there was still interest about where Johnnie Quiet came from and who he was.

As the weeks passed, the tall, thin stranger became a permanent fixture. As well as giving free board and lodgings, Catriona now paid him a small wage. He usually found some carpentry to do as well as odd jobs around the house. "He eats like a bird anyway," Catriona often told friends. "He's not likely to put much of a dent in the household budget. He never seems to spend much money, either."

His main hobby was books. He had joined the library and was a voracious reader. He had very eclectic tastes but anthropology, philosophy and history figured prominently. Books on the Western Isles also attracted him. After Calum came back from school one Friday evening in late November, everyone was in an excited, animated mood because the weekend had arrived and they all sat down to an early dinner in the kitchen. Calum and his mother were tucking in heartily to sausages and mash, Calum's favourite meal. Looking over at Johnnie, Calum couldn't help smiling as he picked at his potato salad and sipped his glass of rainwater. For ease, Catriona now stored some for him in two big bottles in the fridge.

Murdo, Catriona's younger brother, Calum's uncle, had popped round and was eating with them. A thick-set, balding man of average height in his mid thirties, Murdo was a very intelligent school-teacher with a mordant, acerbic, irreverent wit. "I'm glad I'm not a vegetarian like Johnnie," he averred contemptuously. "It sounds more like an eating disorder to me."

Johnnie smiled. "My digestive system is very delicate. If I ate what you eat, I'd die."

"How d'you mean? What makes you so different?"

"Just take my word for it. It's not worth arguing about." Johnny replied testily, obviously wanting the subject dropped. Everyone was watching the news on television. Catriona was knitting, her needles clacking away.

"I wouldn't sit so near the TV, if I were you, Calum," warned Johnnie with a mildly scolding look. "The electro-magnetic waves can be very dangerous."

"Never heard of that one before," said Catriona turning her head with a disbelieving squint in her eye. "Surely the makers would do something about it if that was the case?"

"They haven't discovered it yet," Johnnie stated laconically, without turning his eyes from the television. Calum and his mother exchanged indulgent grins.

It was the twenty-second of November and there was newsreel footage of President Kennedy and his wife arriving by plane in Dallas for a motorcade tour of the city. As soon as this news item started, Johnnie's manner changed very noticeably. Normally calm and unflappable, he looked fidgety and a bit distressed. He pushed his plate to one side. It no longer seemed to interest him.

"Anything wrong, Johnnie?" Catriona asked solicitously.

"Yes. It's going to be a very bad day," he replied sadly, getting up slowly from his seat and leaving his meal unfinished.

"Who for?" asked Calum.

"Everyone. Kennedy in particular." The others looked at each other in puzzlement and Catriona shrugged her shoulders. She was getting used to Johnnie's eccentric, mysterious comments.

He scraped back his chair noisily as he stood up. "I'm going to bed early," Johnnie announced flatly and left the room.

"And I've got to be off," added Murdo, standing up quickly and putting on his car-coat. "I've got loads of homework to mark. Like the labours of Hercules."

Catriona and Calum's relaxed mood changed to horror later in the evening when the news of the assassination came through on the television. Catriona knocked on Johnnie's door to tell him to come and listen but he said he was tired and not feeling too well. The next morning was a Saturday and of course, they were all still shell-shocked from the events the day before. Everyone of that generation would always knows where they were when they heard the stunning news. It was an iconic moment of calamity in history. Understandably, Johnnie's behaviour the evening before had unsettled Calum. Straightaway after breakfast, he raised the subject with him as they did the dishes to help Catriona. Calum was washing with Johnnie drying.

Drying the same plate for the third time, Calum turned his gaze on Johnny. "You knew what was coming, didn't you?"

Johnnie hesitated even more than usual before nodding slightly.

"How?"

After a moment, Johnnie sighed. "Because I can. Let's just leave it at that. Kennedy's murder is a watershed point in history. It was a conspiracy, effectively a coup d'état." He often spoke like an academic. "There are two more tragedies like this to come before the end of the decade. Behind these murders are an evil cabal of very powerful men. Politics in USA has become corrupted by them. Because of their influence, this decade will see the start of a slow destruction of America's democracy. It will degenerate steadily into a plutocracy by the end of the century. But it will be insidious and gradual, so by the time people work it out it's almost too late." Johnny turned and looked Calum steadily in the eyes. "It's the end of innocence for the people when they find out."

He finished drying a cup and put it away.

"We're used to laughing at so-called conspiracy theories and as a result, people are frightened of being ridiculed. When you want to make a theory seem off-the-wall, even if it is cogently argued, call it a conspiracy theory. It helps kill reasoned debate, making the viewpoint seem naively outlandish and it undermines the person who holds the view. The facts of the argument can then be ignored." He shook his head. "This is stupid. In the history of the world, conspiracy has been a huge driver of events. Indeed, it's been the predominant pattern, not a rare aberration.

The cabal will be very successful, virtually invincible and practically irremovable for some time. Their concealed crimes will be horrendous. Corrupt politicians will be on their payroll and the decent ones will be scared to stand up to them, or even expose them, fearing for their careers.......and sometimes, their lives. They also own or control most of the mainstream press, so their crimes won't be made known."

Seeing Calum's doubtful expression, he added, "I can see you find this too extreme to believe. Not in America, eh? Land of the Free and all that. Remember what Edmund Burke said two hundred years ago. "The only thing necessary for evil to triumph is for good men to do nothing." Democracy is a very complex and fragile organism." He picked a wilting rose from a vase on the table. "It's a delicate flower which needs regular watering and continuous supervision. Surprisingly easily, the untended flower can die." Johnny put the flower down on the side of the sink. "What follows is always tyranny and the most cunning kind of tyranny is a hidden one, surreptitiously eating away the core of the political structure from inside. Like a tapeworm. But it can't remain hidden forever. In the end, the scales fall from people's eyes and the truth is laid bare for all to see. This is what will happen in America."

"This also coincides with a separate phenomenon," he continued, piling on the agony. "A great unravelling of the whole of Western society generally, which starts slowly, but gathers speed later."

Calum did not understand. It was all too much to take in. He opened his mouth to ask him to explain, but nothing came out. However, Johnnie answered his unspoken question.

"Civilisations decay from the inside. They destroy <u>themselves</u>. They die from suicide, not murder. What looks like a solid shell falls apart, like teeth that have strong white enamel but are rotten inside. The old empire's steel armour turns to rust. Their enemies only provide the final push. Even the conquering armies themselves are always astounded just how easily and comprehensively the dying empire collapses. Like a huge, pale, floundering, flabby beast with shocked and frightened eyes. It can't understand why its strength went from invincibility to this sorry state. The rise, decline and fall of all empires in history are remarkably consistent."

"You mean history repeats itself?"

"History doesn't repeat, but it rhymes, according to Mark Twain. A very shrewd man. He also said if voting achieved anything, they wouldn't let you do it!"

"Perhaps a wee bit harsh, but there's some truth in it, I suppose."

"Mind you, in dictatorships, it's even worse. The people who cast the votes decide nothing. It's the people who <u>count</u> the votes that decide everything!"

"Touché."

Calum shifted his feet uneasily. He was worried about the future Johnnie was laying out. "Tell me more about what's going to come. It sounds awful," gulped Calum. He could not believe what he was hearing.......who is this strange man? How could he predict the future?

The dishes were finished now and Johnnie was standing, looking out the window with a philosophical, faraway expression. The thousand-yard stare.

Walking towards him at the window, Calum looked very puzzled. "How can you possibly see the future, Johnnie?"

Johnnie crossed his arms, shaking his head slowly. "I only see the past."

"But that wasn't the past you foresaw yesterday. It was the future."

"The future and the past are part of the same river," he said, staring cryptically at the boy.

"I don't understand. Surely, that was the future you saw?"

"It depends where you're standing on the bank."

"I'm confused."

Johnnie cracked a small grin. "Don't worry. That's ok. It proves you're thinking."

With a swish of the hand and a scornful expression, Calum said witheringly, "Ach! This is all gobbledegook to me."

"Of course it is. Shows how little you know about time. For example, we all know that time moves only from past to present to future, don't we? Cause leads to effect. One way traffic." Calum nodded.

"You want some more gobbledegook, then?" he said, craning his neck forward. "In a few decades, a clever scientist will carry out experiments proving that the future actually affects the past! It's totally counter-intuitive, isn't it? And….. very, very frightening. New discoveries are first ridiculed, then violently opposed and finally accepted as self-evident. So, he'll be feverishly vilified by the mainstream scientific establishment and his results trashed. Fifty years after that, it will become as accepted as the law of gravity is today. It'll be called the Law of Retro-Causality. An important scientific innovation rarely makes its way by gradually winning over and converting its opponents. What does happen is that its opponents gradually die out ………..that was Max Planck, by the way. In modern language, you could say the next generation is not lumbered with the ingrained "certainties" of the previous one." He smiled

"With science, today's heresy is tomorrow's truth."

Calum had given up on the conversation.

That evening, Calum was passing Johnnie's room and the door was open. Johnnie was reading a book with a pictorial script on it. Intrigued, the boy asked him what language it was.

"Ancient Norwegian," he replied without looking at him.

When Calum looked at him quizzically, Johnnie merely shrugged. It looked from the cover more like Egyptian hieroglyphics to Calum.

"What's the book about, Johnnie?"

Again, he thought for a couple of seconds, with a smile in his eye.

"It's a kind of history book."

"What kind of history?"

Looking Calum straight in the eye, he said with a very cheeky grin, teasing him,

"A history of the future."

Chapter 2

The winter deepened. However, it was a fairly mild one and Johnnie's benign influence in the household was transforming the family's lives.

One Sunday in early March, over a hearty breakfast of bacon, black pudding and eggs, Catriona said she needed to catch up on a lot of housework and would not be able to go to church with Calum. Would Johnnie mind going along with him? With much hesitation and some persuasion – Johnnie avoided crowds – he agreed to go.

It was one of his mother's little idiosyncrasies. Although she was a Christian, believed in God and encouraged Calum to go regularly, she usually found an excuse for not going herself. Last week, it had been because she had a terrible headache. She did this quite often even before Harry was killed. The truth is the long service bored her, but she didn't want to admit it to Calum – or anyone else for that matter, including herself. Perhaps, a kind of hypocritical, cognitive dissonance, one of life's little mental emollients, oiling the wheels of self-esteem. Human existence wouldn't flow quite so smoothly without such self-delusion. How could you ever criticise others' faults if you had to admit you'd been equally guilty at some point yourself. Ethics would be an arid, pointless concept if we all accepted that literally none of us are able to live up to our own standards. If heroes have feet of clay, what chance have lesser mortals got?

However, the habit of skipping church had become even more common since Harry's death. She was very angry with God. She hadn't forgiven Him for taking Harry away. She couldn't understand why it had to happen.

They both set off with Calum dressed in his best suit. Johnnie didn't have one, so Catriona lent him one of Harry's. It was too baggy for him and he had that uncomfortable, ill-at-ease look that men unused to collars and ties often exhibit. As if they're trussed up in a straitjacket. As Murdo often joked about a teacher friend. "Aye, his suits are made to measure all right. But, sadly….. for someone else."

Both wishing they were somewhere else, they walked to the Free Church on Kenneth Street in the centre of town, a journey of about twenty-five minutes. En route, they passed the football pitch opposite Mitchell's garage. Charlie Barley's the butchers was on the left (Charles H. Macleod to give him his proper name, which no-one ever used). Down Bayhead, past the bowling green and the YMCA, where Calum and his pals often played snooker and table tennis, they turned left up the hill on to Kenneth Street and on the left near the end, they saw the milling throng outside the Free Church. Black and white seagulls wheeled above, loud, throaty "awk's" coming from their bright yellow bills. The air was salty and bracing and a slight drizzle was starting.

All the men were in smart, conservative suits and ties and the younger women were dressed to the nines in classy, fashionable outfits and hats. "You'd think they were going to bloody Royal Ascot," Uncle Murdo often said. The older ones who were widows dressed entirely in black, except perhaps for a white blouse. The atmosphere was positively funereal as the churchgoers, most carrying their own personal bibles, unsmilingly shook hands and spoke in lowered, hushed tones. More like a wake. A sombre Hebridean one, that is, not an Irish one, which is more like a party.

Calum shivered. Not with cold. More like foreboding. He hated the atmosphere of leaden solemnity. The bleak, expressionless faces made his spirit shudder. The dismal dreariness, dreich as a drizzly funeral at twilight. However, his spirits rose a little when just arriving to meet them was Calum's Aunt Alina, a plump, homely 44 year old, with a smile to melt a glacier, the eldest of Catriona's siblings. She too was dressed beautifully and looked very like her sister but plainer, with fancy-rimmed spectacles and a very slight squint in her ice-blue eyes. Luckily, she wasn't one of the gloomy brigade. Her genial disposition prevented this. She was religious and devout but her main enjoyment was eyeing up the women's outfits especially the hats, which she would mentally catalogue and discuss comprehensively with Catriona later.

"Just made it," she panted. "I got delayed." They all entered church straightaway.

Altogether, the service lasted about two and a half hours, consisting of singing half a dozen psalms and saying prayers before a one and a half hour sermon. There was no music at all, with the key for each psalm being set by a "precentor," a member of the congregation whose task it was to lead the singing and set the key. Sounded a bit like a car revving up.

The emphasis was on the Old Testament, sin and repentance. Not a lot of good cheer. About 50 years old, with dark hair greying at the temples, the minister, Reverend Kenneth Macarthur, certainly had tremendous presence despite his short stature and slight build. Like a stern father. To be fair, he was a decent man, virtually a legend on the island, immensely respected by the congregation. An icon in the community. Taking his cue from the others, throughout the whole service, Johnnie was careful to do all the right things at the right time, singing during the psalms and lowering his head during prayers.

Calum was relieved when the service was over, finding it an ordeal, as always. He thought it should become an Olympic event. Since the emphasis would be on extreme stamina, only marathon runners would stand a chance. As they emerged, Murdo walked towards them up the churchyard path in a green Harris tweed jacket and tan cavalry twill trousers. He had come to meet them and give them a lift home to save them the walk. However, Calum suspected a hidden agenda. Murdo wanted to find out Johnnie's views on the service. He was curious about the enigmatic stranger, especially after his forecast about Kennedy. Alina declined a lift as she was visiting a friend in town, so Calum went into the front passenger seat of Murdo's green Morris Minor. Johnnie sat comfortably in the back.

Murdo got to the subject straightaway. "So have you been "born again" then, Johnnie?"

"No, not quite. It's a bit severe for my taste."

Murdo guffawed. "You think that's severe? The Free Church - the "Wee Frees" - broke away from the Church of Scotland in the last century to form their joyless sect. However.........," he said with some relish and emphasis on the second half of the word. "Get this! Some of them decided even the Free Church was too liberal and permissive. Permissive, be damned? So they formed a breakaway group called The Free Presbyterian Church, humorously nicknamed the Wee, Wee Frees. They make the Wee Frees seem like woolly liberals. If it's fire and brimstone with the Wee Frees, it's more like dynamite and plutonium with the Wee, Wee Frees. You're not supposed to breathe on a Sunday, let alone fart. You know why they sing psalms? Because hymns are too bloody jolly. Fun's not a word the Wee Frees understand."

Calum knew Murdo's views and didn't look surprised. Johnnie's eyes wore a slight smile. Murdo had the bit between his teeth, though. "One of their congregation from Luerbost in the Lochs area got a taxi one Sunday to travel to Stornoway to catch the "Loch Seaforth" to the mainland. It leaves at 12.15 am, very early on the Monday morning, by the way, to avoid sailing on Sunday. Even Mammon bows to the Wee Frees on this crazy island. Co-iudh (co-yoo), anyway, as they say, they excommunicated the poor sod for sacrilege. Remember the Sabbath day, to keep it boring. Bloody God-botherers. You'd think they'd give Him a bit of a rest on Sundays. I'm sure He'd appreciate it, since He never gets the chance to put His feet up during the week." Murdo looked away. "I never go to church now, it drives me up the bloody wall. I can't wait to get out. The sermons go on forever. Does me bloody head in. That's why I hate going to places with dark varnished furniture. The smell of it reminds me of the church pews."

He paused for breath. "I'll tell you what the secret of a good sermon is. A good beginning and a good end.....with the two as close together as possible."

Calum bent his head back and laughed loudly. He loved Murdo's rebellious, iconoclastic, world-weary sense of humour. "Aye, the long services certainly remind you what Eternity means. Eternity's a very long time, isn't it, uncle Murdo?" Calum quipped.

"Yeah. Especially towards the end."

Even Johnnie roared with laughter. So Johnnie's starting to develop an appreciation of humour, thought Calum. He may be teaching us all about philosophy, but we're starting to civilise him too. However, Murdo still hadn't finished his tirade. Gradually building his rant to a peak of disgruntlement, he made a zero shape with index finger and thumb.

"Nothing's open on Sunday here. No bars, no cinema, no shops, no restaurants. No anything."

"Apart from the Sailors Home, Uncle Murdo. They have a café the public can use."

"That's true. But nothing else. ....full stop."

"Well, chacun à son gout, as the French say," said Johnnie. "Each one to his own taste. If that's the way they want to worship, that's their choice. Don't forget, religion civilises a society."

"How can all that guilt be civilising?" countered Murdo, with furrowed brow.

"Not if it's overdone. But, without genuine guilt there's no conscience. Without conscience, there's no ethics, no rule of law. And without them, there's no civilisation at all. Only chaos, dog eat dog." Johnnie thought for a moment. "No society can survive without a moral code that's fair and altruistic."

"Surely you can have that without religion?"

Johnnie shook his head. "In theory, but it's fundamentally deficient. Without a belief in a greater reality, it becomes a bleak, cheerless moral code based on bloodless rationality, devoid of any cosmic dimension at all. If you believe in nothing, then your life <u>means</u> nothing. What's more, without religion, science is an orphan, without any perspective. Even more importantly, no-one seems to realise the obvious, that lack of belief in an after-life causes deep-seated, subconscious despair in people. And society in general. To an atheist, what's the purpose of his life? Nothing. Utterly futile, ashes to ashes. Seventy years of a roller-coaster medley of joy, boredom and pain, then bang! You don't exist. You don't even get the chance to look back and think "What was <u>that</u> all about?" This despair is tremendously damaging to society overall. Albert Camus, the French-Algerian author said "To lose one's life is no great matter. When the time comes, I will have the courage to lose mine. But what's intolerable is to see one's life being drained of meaning, to be told there's no reason for existing. A man can't live without some reason for living."

Many famous philosophers have commented on the baleful effect of the growth of atheism in the modern age. Friedrich Nietzsche, the great, often misunderstood, 19th century German philosopher, forecast incredibly accurately the atrocities of the following century caused by atheism. He declared "God is dead. God remains dead. And we have killed him," meaning that humanity had rejected the traditional religious beliefs that had been the bedrock of society for many centuries. He did not believe in a God himself, but he recognized the logical result of the dismantling of this formidable, traditional structure of values would be an upsurge of both nihilism and totalitarianism. He forecast communist revolutions disrupting the world and major wars in which millions would die. Let's face it, his predictions were absolutely spot-on and it's hard to fault his logic. Dostoyevsky, Nietzsche's contemporary, by contrast a devout Russian Orthodox Christian, came to the same conclusion, with great sadness and regret. "If God does not exist, everything is permissible." The early 20th century psychologist and philosopher, Carl Jung, believed that Mankind is incapable of creating a viable, enduring, humane system of values on his own."

"Well, crikey, that's a bloody depressing way of looking at things," observed Murdo, putting on an exaggerated long face. "Actually, one of the other teachers at my school likes to hedge his bets on religion. He says he doesn't really believe in an afterlife, but he always carries a change of underwear. Just in case."

Johnnie ignored the joke. He enjoyed Murdo's buoyant humour, normally, but he was talking about serious things and the flippant interruption irritated him for once. Looking directly at Murdo, he stated with mild defiance, "I refuse to believe life is just a huge cosmic coincidence. A sick joke without any meaning."

Everyone was silent in thought. Then Johnnie turned to Calum.

"H.G. Wells said that if God doesn't exist, nothing matters; however, if He does exist, nothing else matters. That one certainly hits the spot, doesn't it?"

"So you obviously believe in God, then?"

"Yes, where I'm from, nearly everyone believes in a Supreme Spirit."

"Why?"

"Look at a butterfly's wing...... or a fly's eye. Tiny things, yet they're so incredibly complex. Look how things in the universe are interrelated. Everything's connected to everything else. If that's not deliberate, intelligent design, I don't know what is. "But….." he said emphasising the conjunction, "like you, we don't know for certain what the afterlife is like. In fact, what the Grand Purpose of it all is. We're all victims of a benign conspiracy."

"Why benign?" said Murdo with a raised eye-brow.

"Look around you." Johnnie said, raising his arms in front of him. "At the joys of nature and life."

"And what about the sorrows?"

"Without them, we couldn't appreciate the pleasures. Without evil, goodness would be meaningless with no yard-stick to go on. There would be nothing to strive for, or fight against. What's more, our souls wouldn't grow. Life is meant to teach us new things. The world is a school-house and we wouldn't learn anything if life was all a bowl of cherries. Permanently sunbathing by a sparkling, limpid, swimming pool being served cocktails. Remember that there's no sun without shadow, no day without night and to understand life, you need to understand both."

"Why's everything hidden from us, then?"

"Presumably, we're not meant to know for certain. For example, if people knew, it might frighten them into morality."

"What's wrong with that?"

"Well, you have to decide to act well for the most important reason of all. Because it's right. Not because you'll be rewarded in the afterlife. Doing good is only a virtue if you choose it freely for its own sake."

"Free will and all that?"

"Absolutely. Without free will, everything is meaningless. Just a predetermined series of events over which you have no control, where you don't make the choices......with no spiritual or moral significance whatsoever."

After a moment, Johnnie changed the subject. "What's the political flavour round here? Labour? Conservative?"

"Solid Labour." said Murdo. "They'd vote for a rhesus monkey if he had a red rosette. I've voted Labour myself in the past but they're starting to get complacent. Taking the voters for granted. I wouldn't be surprised if the nationalists gain ground in the future."

"I read somewhere that our MP's got one of the worst attendance records in the House," said Calum, who knew more about current affairs than most adults.

"Yeah, that's right," grinned Murdo, "Martin Bormann turns up more often than he does."

Murdo dropped them off at home and drove back to his own house in Torquil Terrace, not far away. After lunch, they all went and sat in the living room. Johnnie saw that both Calum and Catriona were subdued and after a few gentle questions, they admitted they were still depressed by Harry's death. The two of them had stopped talking to each other about it. The memories were too raw. Too many tears shed. They were repressing their pain.

"If you discussed it a bit more, it might help. Depression thrives on silence," Johnnie ventured. Gingerly, with some trepidation, he added, "Where I come from, I'm a trained counsellor. Will you give it a go?"

Catriona gave a despairing shrug and turned her eyes blankly to the window. The look said "I don't really care, but ok." Calum nodded. A kind of indifferent acquiescence.

"Tell me about your dad."

"He was great. A fantastic dad, always there for me. Huge personality. I've never met anyone like him. He was really great with my sister Kathy too. Fought hard to get the education department to finally accept she needed to go to a special school for the deaf. Originally they said she'd be ok in an ordinary school. No way." Calum lowered his head not wanting another man to see his mouth quiver and his eyes fill up. "He was my hero. I'll never ever be his equal. Until the day I die."

Catriona felt a sympathetic ache in the pit of her stomach - as if she'd been punched. She felt for her son. She sensed what he was going through. It was probably even worse for Kathy, who felt totally bereft without her dad.

"Catriona, what about you?"

"Well, where do I start?" she sighed, turning to look at Johnnie, the raw pain evident in her eyes. "He was posted to the island in 1943 with the RAF. The Leodhasachs, (Lee-oh-sachs), the Lewis people, are great when you get to know them, but they can be very queer and clannish with outsiders at first. Especially Sassenachs, because of all the old historical baggage.........."

"Sassenachs are Englishmen," translated Calum, interrupting his mother with a wink at Johnnie.

".......but he won them all round with his strength of character and his way with people. He could charm the birds off the trees. Calum got a bit of this from his dad too, I notice."

Calum forced a wan smile.

"I met him at a dance in Stornoway. He looked good in his RAF uniform and he was quite handsome." She got up, poked the peat fire and walked to the window.

"Didn't it put you off? Him being a.......Sassenach, I mean?" queried Johnnie.

Looking into the garden, she replied with a pronounced shake of the head. "Not in the least, I'm not like that. Take people as I find them. I think I get that from my father. Certainly not my mother, though. My mother, Kate, had a very dominant personality and was dead against him. Told everyone she couldn't stick her daughter going out with that heathen Englishman. Really rude to him, she was.

At the very beginning, she wouldn't have him in the house. Although she mellowed a bit after a month or two, she still wasn't very welcoming. Luckily, Harry got on really well with my father. Alec was a quiet, dignified, unassuming man and there was a huge mutual respect between them. I think Harry would have given up on the family if it hadn't been for my dad."

"Dad never gave up," protested Calum vehemently. "If he was determined about something, he would never give in. No one would beat him. That was one of his best qualities."

Catriona nodded sympathetically.

"He's a god to you, Calum. I know. Quite right too, he was a wonderful father, but I'm worried it's giving you an inferiority complex. He was a great man but he had his faults too, you know. He could be very hard on you. Expected a lot. You mustn't turn him into a paragon and let his memory crush you."

Calum shrugged sourly.

"Harry never ever forgave my mother. After we got engaged, my mother changed her tune. She saw she'd massively misjudged him and went totally the opposite way. She'd grown to like and respect him a lot. Despite the way she treated him at first, she was normally a hospitable woman by nature. She had a good heart and was very good to her family. Including you, Calum. You always stuck up for your dad. He never hid his dislike of my mother from you, which he should have done. It put you off your granny a wee bit, which is not right. She was very generous to you and Kathy. Spoiled you both a bit too. Although Harry was pleasant enough to her in company, he literally never had a good thing to say about her to me. I spent my short married life trying to get him to accept her and see her good qualities. But he never would."

Catriona looked down disconsolately. "It was very hard for me." She ran her fingers through her hair. "If you're wondering why there's no tears, it's because I'm all "cried out." For the first.... I don't know.... three months or so, I cried all the time. I thought I'd never stop. But I did. I just couldn't carry on like that. What's left now is just loneliness and despair. A hollow.... emptiness." She couldn't believe all this emotion was coming out. It felt like she was releasing a knot of tension from her mind.

There was a hiatus for many seconds as they all thought about Catriona's words.

Catriona continued. "Before the war, Harry was assistant works manager in a wool-spinning factory in West Yorkshire, where he came from. It's a woollen area. All his family were connected with wool. His father and eldest brother were dyers. Two other brothers, Raymond and Willie, were self-employed tailors and his other brother, Hubert, was in shoddy."

"What's that?" asked Johnnie.

"They take old clothes and strip them back to the fibres. It makes poor quality clothing, so instead they make sacks and cheap clothing items out of them. I'm not sure if that's the origin of the word shoddy or if it's the other way round. Maybe the cloth's called shoddy because it's poor quality. Anyway, it doesn't really matter," she said, "After the war, Harry got a job here as manager of a tweed mill for a while, but he got offered a fantastic job in 1949 through a friend's recommendation as works manager of BMK, a big carpet manufacturer in Kilmarnock in Ayrshire. You know the "jumping lamb" trademark? You were only three years old, Calum. We thought long and hard. But we decided to go for it in the end.

Until we bought a house, they put us in one of the company houses in Mount Avenue. I loved that house. Very airy and plenty of room."

"So did I," interjected Calum. "It had a big garden with lots of fruit trees and berry bushes. Myself and my pals used to play in it for hours."

"We were very happy as a family in Kilmarnock," continued Catriona. "However, in 1958, Harry sacked one of the foremen he thought was a lazy troublemaker. Unfortunately, he was a trade union leader and the work-force came out on strike. Instead of sticking up for your dad, the directors panicked and re-instated the foreman. Harry left. By mutual consent, shall we say. That was a turning point in his life. He was disillusioned and he'd developed duodenal ulcers with the stress. He vowed that day he'd never work for anyone again. And he never did.

We sold up and came back here. Using his settlement from BMK, he started a one man wholesale business supplying provisions to grocers' shops. He got a lucky break early on when he got the Baxter's agency for the West Highlands and Islands. Baxter's is a very popular, Scottish luxury brand sold all over Britain and abroad. Although he was born in an industrial area, his hobbies when he was young were all outdoor ones. Hill-walking mainly. Harry always loved Lewis."

"Wasn't that a bit of a culture shock for you, Calum," said Johnnie, "after living in a big town on the mainland all your life bar the first three years?"

"No, not at all. From the age of five, every year I'd been packed off on the plane from Glasgow for the whole of the summer holidays to stay with granny and grandad in Portrona Drive in Stornoway. I loved it. Mum and Dad used to come up for the last two weeks, my father's fortnight summer holiday. So, although I was sad to leave my pals in Killie behind, and going to Kilmarnock football matches as well, I was very happy to move to Stornoway."

"It took Harry a lot of really hard work to build the business up," Catriona cut in. "Being an outsider and all that and no experience of the provisions trade. Also, although he was very clever, his admin was always a total mess." She smiled inside as she remembered the disorganised piles of paper-work that Harry professed were "filing."

"But.....as Calum says, he had an engaging way with him." She sighed. "He was a gentleman and scrupulously straight in business too. He had very high standards of good behaviour in life generally but he also had a fantastic sense of humour. Laughed a lot. He had a quick temper too, though. Not physically violent in any way, but really sharp verbally. When he was angry, or he thought you'd let him down, he let you know. I've never known anyone who could give a person a dressing-down as well as Harry. Cool and incisive."

Calum cut in. "Yeah, when Dad told you off, you knew you'd been told off. But although he was quick to anger, once he'd said his piece, that was it. He'd literally be joking with me thirty seconds later. Mum couldn't understand the speed of the change and used to smile and shake her head at him in disbelief. I really liked that about him. Luckily, I've inherited this trait from him. I'm exactly the same, which I'm glad of. Holding grudges is a pointless exercise. Unless it's something really serious, of course."

Johnnie nodded. "You know what Kennedy said about holding grudges. He said you should always forgive your enemies. But never forget their names."

This raised a chuckle and Catriona carried on. "You mustn't forget, the Leodhasachs may be clannish and wary of strangers at first, but they'll give you a chance if you try hard enough. They know a decent person when they get to know them. Once they'd seen his mettle, they really took to him. You should have seen the number of people at the funeral. The church was full and there were still loads of people outside who couldn't get in."

Catriona's eyes dropped again. Turning his head, Calum looked out the window and sniffed back a tear.

"Don't get me wrong," she said after a long pause to recover, "he didn't see the islanders through rose-tinted glasses. Although he liked them a lot, he saw their foibles too. "Bottles and bibles," he used to say, "they'll be the death of this ruddy place, if they don't watch." He drank very little himself and he wasn't a great fan of the Free Church."

"Was he religious at all?" asked Johnnie.

"To a degree. He believed in a life after death and he was brought up C. of E. but he only went to church for matches and dispatches."

Johnnie angled his head to one side and screwed up his eyes questioningly.

"Funerals and weddings," she explained.

"Tell me about your grandad, Calum. Sounds like a nice man."

"He was the foreman at Forsyth's Bakery in Francis Street. He started at four in the morning and came back home for his breakfast for an hour at eight. He finished work at one o'clock in the afternoon. If I wasn't out playing with my pals, I'd run down Macaulay Road to meet him coming back. Without fail, every day, he brought me back either an orange or an apple. I never saw him lose his temper and he very rarely told me off for anything. I liked him so much, I would never have done anything to anger him anyway. When I was very young, I'd sit on his knee and he'd slowly peel the fruit, cut it into bite-size pieces and hand it to me. It's funny how you remember small, insignificant things, but one of them was the smell of flour from his tweed jacket. He had white hair and a bald head. When I touched his bald head, there was a very thin, almost invisible, dusty film of flour on it. He had endless patience and taught me to read when I was four before I started going to school from the "Black Bob" comic-strip in the "Weekly News." It's about a shepherd and his sheep-dog. We used to read it together. I can see why Dad liked him so much. He had a quiet....sort of.... serenity and dignity about him.

There was something, though, which Mum never saw. They argued a lot. Grannie used to nag him all the time when no other adults were there. In a nasty way. They always spoke in Gaelic when they were on their own, so I only caught the gist of it. Grown-ups always act as if young kids aren't there or don't understand. However, I picked up the atmosphere very well. It disturbed me. I felt so sorry for grand-dad and I couldn't understand why she did it. I also couldn't work out why he put up with it. It certainly wasn't a marriage made in heaven." He looked at his mother. "Grannie didn't have ulcers herself, but she was a carrier."

Ignoring her son's flippant remark, Catriona mildly protested. "I think you're exaggerating a bit, Calum," She didn't like her mother being criticised. Cheering up, and changing the subject, she turned to Johnnie. "You know what? As usual you're absolutely right, Johnnie Quiet. This has helped get things out in the open and I feel better for it. We couldn't have done this until recently. It would have been too raw."

Calum nodded vigorously and mother and son embraced for some time before breaking away. It was the first time for some weeks. Catriona thought to herself that Johnnie had yet another ability. She marvelled at the breadth of his personal qualities. After a few seconds, she said "I'm going to make a cup of tea."

Johnnie laughed. "....And I'm going to try a weak tea without milk. It seems to give everyone else here such comfort. There must be something about it."

"Aye, did you know it's a natural antiseptic too, so that should appeal to your health-conscious soul."

Chapter 3

A few weeks later on a Saturday morning, Catriona walked down to Charles H. Macleod's, the butchers. Less than ten minutes journey. Charlie Barley, as he was always known to everyone, was smartly dressed as usual in white shirt and tie with a crisp, clean butcher's apron on top. He had black hair and sported a neatly-trimmed pencil moustache. He looked very dapper.

"Charlie, give me a couple of your black marags, please."

As he turned to go to the fridge for the black puddings, Charlie raised his eyebrows.

"I thought you made your own, Catriona."

"I do, but I've been too busy recently. We're all going to see my uncle Dolligan in Callanish today and I always bring some black pudding. Yours are the next best to mine."

Charlie tilted his head backwards, letting out a hearty laugh. "I suppose I'm meant to take that as a compliment then, Catriona?"

"You bet. You got it in one," she replied with just the faintest flicker of a smile. She was proud of her own home-made marags. Calum loved them too, but he admitted his Grannie's were the best he'd ever tasted. Since Catriona actually agreed with him, she wasn't too put out.

On returning home, she made everyone a very light breakfast. Said they'd better not eat too much. "These country folk are so generous they always give you far too much to eat."

Calum nodded in agreement. "And they get insulted if you don't scoff the lot."

Nodding in the direction of an armchair in the corner, Catriona continued, "Calum's Uncle Murdo's coming with us. Johnnie, why don't you join us too? It's a nice village and they're great hosts. Callanish is on the west side of the island about 14 miles from here. Next to Loch Roag."

Everyone got into Catriona's dark blue Vauxhall Velox and she drove off through Marybank on the road to Callanish with Murdo in the front passenger seat. Perceval Road is in the Manor Park area, right on the edge of Stornoway and very quickly they were in the countryside. They left the whirling gulls behind in return for the slight smell of heather and peat. Lewis perfume. The only sound was a slight wailing of the wind through a slightly opened window, Johnnie was looking intently out of the window and Calum wondered what he thought of the Lewis landscape. It would seem very alien to someone from mainland Britain, he mused, let alone a foreign country. Not mountainous at all, except in the southern part of Lewis on the border with Harris, where the low hills start to expand significantly into much higher ground in Harris.

The terrain essentially comprises very rocky, treeless moorland. Heather-covered peat-bogs dotted with craggy outcrops of grey rocks partly covered with patches of lime-coloured lichen. Small lochs pepper the landscape. The locals would certainly never die of thirst. Every so often, a flock of sheep was scattered over the turf. A few plump, white-faced Cheviots, with tightly curled woollen fleeces, but mainly scrawny, black-faced Lewis sheep with sparse, straggly fleeces. Apparently, for Harris Tweed, for which the island is famous, you need a mix of wools. Possibly, Calum thought, the Cheviot gives softness and richness, but he didn't know enough about it to be sure. Yarn from the Lewis wool would perhaps give hardiness and durability. Not unlike the islanders themselves.

Murdo eyed Johnnie. "I read somewhere that the commonest rock on the island, Lewisian gneiss, is the oldest type known to Man."

"Yes, it's very wild here, isn't it, Johnnie?" added Catriona.

"Rugged and bare. Not lush," he agreed, inadvertently echoing Calum's earlier thoughts. "But it has its own beauty and charm……………..like the people."

"How do you mean?"

"Unpretentious and forthright."

Flattery wasn't Johnnie's normal style. He said things as they are. He'd never make a PR man. Trying to hide her slight embarrassment at the unexpected compliment, Catriona cut in quickly,

"Although you might not be saying that if it was a stormy winter's day with squally, freezing rain driving into your face. Today's very mild for the time of year." Johnnie responded wordlessly with that easy, whimsical smile they had all grown to like.

Actually, it was mild for early March. Although it can get very raw, wild and stormy at the drop of a hat, irrespective of the season, the average temperature is not nearly as low as the latitude suggests, because the island is right in the path of the Gulf Stream. That Saturday was dry with a fairly strong, cold, but not icy wind. Above their heads was a typical Hebridean sky. Four seasons competing at once, a coat of many colours. "If you don't like the weather, wait about twenty minutes - another one will come along," as the old saying goes. Swirls of slate-grey cloud rolled in an otherwise egg-shell blue sky. The sort of day when the Celtic weather god couldn't quite make up his mind whether to smile or gnash his teeth.

The light in the Highlands and Islands is different from the rest of Britain. It's pale and subtle, with a clean, translucent, liquid quality. A limpid, delicate, watercolour light. Like an impressionist painting but not in oils. That wouldn't be the right medium. Too garish and brash.

Taking his cue from Catriona, Murdo turned to Johnnie. "We have a secret way of predicting the weather here."

"Really?" said Johnnie.

"Aye. If you can see the mainland, it's going to rain….." Murdo paused for effect.

"And if you can't?" asked Johnnie, rising to the bait.

"…..then it's already raining."

No matter how many times he heard Murdo tell that hoary old joke, Calum always raised a smile at it.

In the 1960's, although the country roads outside Stornoway were good and very well tarmac-ed, most were one-track with passing places to allow traffic to pass from the other direction.

Looking at Johnnie in the mirror, Catriona explained, "Just to let you know who we're going to see. My uncle Dolligan's about 70. His real name's Donald but he's always had that nickname since he was a lad. Don't know why. He's my mother's brother and he inherited the family house in Callanish," adding proudly, "He fought in the First World War, became a sergeant and won the Military Medal. After he came back, he got a job working in MacBrayne's shipping office; then he retired when he was 65. His two older brothers, Norman and Alan, died at Paschendale. The grief nearly blinking killed my granny. Lots of Lewismen died in the Forces. more than in any other small area of the UK. As a result, an unusual custom arose from it. I don't think it happened elsewhere. I've never seen it anywhere else anyway. A lot of nieces were called after their dead uncles by adding "a" or "ina" to their name." Nodding at Calum, "Your Aunt Alina was called after Alan and, as you know, my middle name is Normanna after the other brother."

"Aye, and about 10 years ago," said Murdo with a smirk, "Dolligan got the "curam.""

Catriona flashed her eyes angrily at him. Turning to Johnnie, Murdo expanded. "It's a Hebridean thing. It means they go all religious. They're "born again." After leading a wild, boozy life, they suddenly start ending all their sentences with "if we're spared.""

Catriona's face reddened. "Don't be so cynical, Murdo!" she erupted angrily. She was fed up always having to defend her uncle's religious conversion to her brother. "He wasn't that wild when he was young and he's very genuine about his beliefs. He was brave during the war too."

"Mach a seo! (mach a shaw) Get away with you!" he replied with a sarcastic glare. "He liked a good dram as much as anyone. It's only fire insurance he's after. Against the fires of hell. You know what I mean..... the one specially reserved for the Wee Frees," scoffed Murdo with a dismissive swipe of the hand. "But, yes, ok, I do respect him for his courage in the war. It's just his holier-than-thou attitude I dislike. Reminds me of what Disraeli said about Gladstone. "I don't really mind him always having the ace of trumps hidden up his sleeve. What I can't take is his claim that God put it there.""

"Very droll, Murdo," Catriona said with equal sarcasm. "For all that, he speaks well of you, even although you're such a boorish, bloody heathen. And he puts up with all your mickey-taking in good spirit." Murdo couldn't hide a cheeky grin. He loved to wind his sister up. A rebel without a cause, as they say. He actually got on very well with Dolligan but religious fervour disturbed him. Too many Sundays as a kid forced to sit through yet another droning monologue and diatribe.

"Anyway, how can you be so hoity-toity about Dolligan being wild when he was young? Which he wasn't. You were much worse than him."

This was true. Murdo should have walked through his history degree at Aberdeen University. He was extremely intelligent and well read, but he only scraped through after a re-sit. He was too fond of wine, women and song – and singing wasn't really the problem. At the beginning of his final year, he went as usual to deposit his grant cheque for the term in the Aberdeen Savings Bank. The young teller, who knew Murdo's spending habits well by then, asked without a hint of a smile, "Would you like it all out now, sir, or do you want to leave some in for the afternoon?" Even Murdo had to admire the young lad's cheek. Luckily, he saw the funny side of it and they both doubled up with laughter.

Murdo had been just too young to fight in the Second World War and wished he'd had the chance to do so. After doing his National Service in the late 1940's he went through college. "Aye, through the front door an' kicked oot the back" as one of his Aberdonian drinking pals used to say. Qualifying as a primary teacher, he now worked at a small school just outside Stornoway. Although he still liked a drink and a night out, he now kept it within reasonable bounds. He'd grown up. The pupils christened him "Prof" because he was so well-read, particularly in history. He'd never married and had only recently come out of a five-year relationship with a girl from Stornoway.

Catriona was disappointed at the way the conversation was going. "Why are you always such a cynic, Murdo?"

"I'm not a cynic. I'm a realist."

"Oh yeah? What's the difference?"

"A realist is a cynic that's been proved right."

They all had to laugh at that one, which dispersed the adversarial atmosphere.

In about twenty-five minutes, they arrived at the small village of Callanish, where Catriona's mother had been born and brought up. A congenial, mild smell of peat smoke coming from all the house-chimneys was carried on the stiff breeze. Climbing the small winding hill, the car pulled up outside the house. As they went to the door,

Dolligan's wife, Mairi was there to meet them with a beaming smile. "Come in, I've got dinner ready." Like most working-class Scots, she called lunch "dinner." Mairi was below average height, with a happy face and a grey bun in her hair. She was very spry and fast-moving for an overweight lady in her late 60's. Although born and bred on the island, she had worked as a nurse in Glasgow for many years until she met Dolligan when she was on holiday back in Stornoway. They got married in their forties and therefore had no children. However, they were a very happy, easy-going couple. Murdo's description of Dolligan was a bit of an exaggeration, although he was very religious and wore it on his sleeve to some degree.

The house was an adapted tigh dubh (tie doo), "black house" in English. Strongly built of local stone without cement, it originally had a turf and thatch roof with two large rooms. In the 1930's, a second storey with two bedrooms and a bathroom was built and a strong pitched felt roof was added.

Catriona entered first, followed by Calum and Murdo bending slightly through the very low doorway. Finally, Johnnie came in, stooping even more, his eyes taking in the surroundings.

"So this is Johnnie Quiet then, is it?" said Dolligan with a warm smile that seemed to cover his whole face. "We've heard so much about you. Come in and make yourself at home. As my dad used to say to welcome visitors, "Relax, you're at your grannie's."" As Catriona handed the marags to Mairi, Johnnie's eyes roamed round, taking in the details of the living room. It was a welcoming, homely room, with a roaring peat fire on his right. The mild, but pleasant, aromatic smell of it pervaded the room. There was a large couch, three easy chairs and a table with eight armless, wooden chairs. On the uneven, white distempered stone walls were some family photographs as well as framed religious sayings, such as "Trust in God" and "Remember the Sabbath Day, to keep it holy." In one corner, there was a china cabinet with some fancy china and silverware. A small book-case filled another corner with a bible resting on a small side-table next to Dolligan's armchair.

Johnnie shook hands with Dolligan, a short, sparely built man with a shock of thick, wavy, ungovernable, salt-and-pepper grey hair sitting atop a craggy, angular, weather-beaten face. He was wearing a pair of russet-brown Harris tweed trousers and matching waistcoat over a blue and white striped shirt with an open-necked granddad collar.

Turning to the sheepdog collie in the far corner, Dolligan beckoned him over. "Glen, come and say hello to Johnnie." However, Glen sat rigidly with a wary, alert look in his eye. "Can't understand it. He normally greets everyone with his tail wagging all the time. You must have put the wrong after-shave on today." However, the dog didn't want to know. He sat motionless and never took his eyes off Johnnie until he left the house. Like all animals, he sensed Johnnie was different from the others and it unsettled him.

"Dinner's ready. Bong," announced Mairi immediately, pretending to hit an imaginary gong with an imaginary drumstick.

After they had all sat down at the table, Mairi served up the first course, a delicious Scotch broth made with Lewis mutton, vegetables and pearl barley. As Mairi explained, Lewis mutton has a lovely sweet flavour since the sheep live on heather, adding, "It's less fatty, too." Having seen the physically unimpressive, skinny, scraggy, black-faced Lewis sheep, Johnnie thought it was no wonder. Obviously, there's always a silver lining.

Before they started eating, Dolligan, at the head of the table, started to say grace. In Gaelic. However, as always, he droned on for fully four or five minutes in a very slow, sanctimonious, old-fashioned way, punctuated at the end of each sentence with a smacking of the lips. Just when it looked as if he had finished, a new sentence would appear. Calum and Murdo thought grace was never going to end. Steadfastly refusing to close his eyes during the prayer, Murdo merely lowered his head slightly as a sop to propriety. He winked across at Calum, then raised his eyes slowly to the ceiling in mock resignation. Catriona narrowed her eyes and glared at both of them.

They were all relieved when the word "Amen" finally arrived. After a few seconds silence, Mairi broke the spell. "He's always the same, bless him. He gets caught up with it all."

Not unpleasantly and with a smile, Murdo added, "Aye, it's more like the Gettysburg Address …..and the soup's always cold by the time he's finished as well." Dolligan did not look put out at the gentle teasing and the flutter of mirth relieved the slight tension.

Sitting forward in his chair, Johnnie said with a frown, "I notice you said grace in Gaelic, but most people speak English most of the time, don't they?"

Murdo answered for Dolligan. "Up until about fifty years ago, nearly everyone was bilingual, although some country people like my granny spoke only Gaelic. Nowadays, it depends mainly on two things. Where you come from on the island and what generation you are. Outside Stornoway, Dolligan's generation learnt only Gaelic until they went to school at five years old where they then learnt English. They were taught in English too. Although English then became dominant overall for the rest of their lives, country people tended to talk to each other in Gaelic. And most still do.

However, in Stornoway, English has always been dominant since about the turn of the century. The number of Gaelic speakers amongst young townies is dropping very fast. Some have picked it up from their parents, but most of Calum's school pals in Stornoway don't speak Gaelic at all. Calum only has some words and phrases in Gaelic, isn't that right?"

Calum nodded. "Aye, it's a shame really. Mum and Alina speak it fluently but with Dad being English it wasn't spoken in the house. I did pick up quite a bit though, listening to the family. I actually know quite a few words and phrases, but because I don't know the grammar and the tenses and that sort of thing, I can't string sentences together."

After Mairi had removed the soup plates, she replaced them with dinner plates and large serving-dishes full of boiled mutton from the soup, as well as dishes of steaming boiled potatoes, carrots, turnips and brussels sprouts. Johnnie contented himself with the vegetables.

"Calum says you've got the second sight," said Dolligan, spearing a sprout. Seeing Johnnie's questioning, raised eyebrows, he explained "You can see the future."

Johnnie immediately shot a stern, accusing glance at Calum. He obviously wasn't pleased. He liked to keep a low profile. Calum looked away guiltily. Reading the situation, Dolligan went on, "Och, for goodness' sake, don't worry about that, Johnnie. We're used to second sight on this island. It's part of the Gaelic heritage. Didn't you know that? Plenty of people have it." Turning to Catriona, "Look at old Shuggie, Hughie Morrison the weaver, at the other end of the village. He's always predicting all sorts of things."

"Nostradamus was the greatest prophet of all time," announced Calum, who loved a mystery." I've read all his predictions. It's fascinating trying to unravel what he's saying."

"That's true." chipped in Murdo, "but Lewis has its very own Nostradamus, the Brahan Seer."

"Who's he?" enquired Johnnie, his interest pricked.

"I think you mean "Who *was* he?"corrected Dolligan, knocking out the dottle from his pipe into an ashray and going through the laborious process that pipe-smokers do to refill their pipes. Mairi cleared the table, knowing a story was coming. Calum loved when Dolligan told stories. He was a master at it. He always thought Dolligan should be on the radio or television telling stories. A new programme, called Mac-Jackanory.

"Well, now. Let's begin at the beginning. His name was Kenneth Mackenzie, nicknamed Coinneach Odhar (<u>Cuhn</u>-yach <u>Oh</u>-ar) in Gaelic and he was born in the Uig area of Lewis in the early 17th century. His story's well-known all over Scotland - and beyond. He was a simple man from a very poor family. The story goes that late one summer evening, his mother was seeing to the cattle on the sheiling – a summer pasture - near the graveyard in the village of Baile-na-Cille (Bahl-na-keel), when she saw ghosts rising from every grave and setting off in all directions, returning about an hour later. She was afraid and fascinated at the same time. A few minutes after the others had returned, she saw that one grave was still open and soon its occupant, a fair, teenage girl appeared, hurrying through the air to her grave. Kenneth's mother was still a bit afraid but very curious so she plucked up her courage and decided to be bold, placing her distaff over the entrance to the grave. She'd heard somewhere this would stop a ghost from re-entering its grave.

The ghost asked her to remove the distaff but Kenneth's mother answered that she would do so only when the girl told her what was going on.

The ghost sighed. "Once a year, we're all allowed to return for a short while to where we came from."

"So why did you return so late after the others?"

"Because I had further to go than them. I was the daughter of the King of Norway but I drowned swimming near the beach. Very sad. My body was carried far over the sea and washed ashore near here. I was buried here by the local people."

She looked at the old lady directly.

"Since your compatriots gave me a Christian burial, I'll give you something in return. Go over to that small loch. Near the edge you'll find a small, shiny, blue stone with a hole in the middle. Give it to your son and he will gain the power of prophecy. By looking through the hole, he will see future events."

Everyone's eyes were transfixed on the storyteller. Dolligan took a long puff on his pipe and relit it with a match. The pipe-filling interruptions added a little bit of theatre to the whole procedure, punctuating the story in all the right places. Catriona loved the rich, slightly fruity aroma of Dolligan's cherry Sobranie tobacco.

"Sounds like a strange stone to me," said Mairi.

"Yes." added Johnnie, who had been silent, enthralled by the story. "Stones can have <u>very</u> strange properties indeed," he added cryptically.

Dolligan carried on, ignoring the exchange. He loved telling stories. This is a great tradition in Lewis going right back to time immemorial. In the long days of summer, the crofters and their families worked long, extended hours. In the winter, however, they only worked the short hours of light. On the long dark evenings, with the wind howling and rain angrily battering the strong, thick walls, they would all gather together round a blazing peat fire, warm and relaxed, drinking tea and often whisky, telling strange, supernatural tales. The candle-light and flickering flames would cast eerie shadows on the walls, heightening the scary atmosphere.

"So," went on Dolligan portentously, smacking his lips. "Young Kenneth gained his second sight and became well known in the island for his strange powers. Soon his exploits reached the ears of the owner of the island at the time, the Earl of Seaforth, who gave him a job at his estate on the mainland, at Brahan near Inverness. Kenneth's abilities became legendary and he was feted by the Earl and his wife, often consulting him on the future and showing him off at parties with their friends. A kind of diverting entertainment for their posh pals."

"What did he predict? Was he accurate?" asked Johnnie.

"You bet. Very accurate. He predicted the building of the Caledonian Canal, as well as the arrival of cars, electricity and gas.

The Highlands would be criss-crossed with a multitude of roads, he said, with a dramshop on every corner. Also, he knew one day there would be a great battle on Culloden Moor, where many Highlanders would die."

Murdo, whose hobby was history, added, "Another prediction was that a day would come when a king came to the throne who would never be crowned. When this happened, there would be troublesome times. Edward the Eighth fits this description. He abdicated in 1936 before his coronation - and three years later the Second World War began."

Lots of nodding in agreement from the group.

"What did he say about Lewis?" asked Calum, who had often heard the Brahan Seer's story but loved to hear it repeated, enjoying the mystery and intrigue of it all.

"The island will be laid waste by a destructive war. The invading army will drive the Leodhasachs back all the way down to Tarbert in Harris, killing many people on the way. However, they will be turned back and defeated by the bravery of a left-handed Macleod."

"It would have to be a Macleod, wouldn't it, Dolligan?" joked Murdo.

Undeterred, Dolligan continued "The seer made lots of other eerie predictions for the future." He started to rise slowly from his chair. "Let me get my book out to read them accurately." Instead, Mairi got up, took a well-thumbed green book from the book-case beside her and handed it to her husband. Perching a pair of wire-rimmed reading glasses half way down his nose, he raised his head. Looking down his nose at the page, he continued. "Yes, this is a good one. It says: "The people will emigrate to islands now unknown, but which yet will be discovered in the boundless oceans. After that, the deer and other wild animals shall be exterminated and browned by horrid black rains. The whole country will be so utterly desolated and depopulated that the crow of a cock shall not be heard north of

Drum-uachdair. Later, the people will return and take undisturbed possession of the lands of their ancestors.""

"I wonder what the black rains will be?" asked Calum excitedly. "Acid rain, maybe.......or nuclear fall-out, even?"

"Och, don't get too carried away," tut-tutted Murdo. "It's only a prophecy. Anyway, I don't think we'll ever get a nuclear war. The Russkis know they'd end up as toast if they start one. So, it ain't gonna happen."

Johnnie eyed Murdo with a serious expression. "So you're not really interested in nuclear war, then?"

"Nah......not really."

Johnnie continued to look Murdo directly in the eye. Speaking slowly and evenly, he said with great clarity, "That's a pity. It's very interested in you."

Murdo shifted uncomfortably in his chair. Although he liked Johnnie, he found some of his comments very unsettling. He had a habit of hitting the nail uncomfortably on the head.

"Anyway," said Dolligan, "getting back to the seer." Reading from the book again, he quoted, "As Kenneth became more famous, he also became a little arrogant and he had a vindictive tongue when he wanted. He was no respecter of rank.

One day, Lady Seaforth was entertaining some of her well-bred, aristocratic friends with Kenneth acting as an interesting side-show. Her husband was in Paris on a diplomatic mission and had not returned when he said he would. She asked Kenneth where he was at this time and why he was delayed. Looking into the stone, Kenneth let out a quiet snigger.

"Don't worry, he's fit and well and enjoying himself."

When asked to explain, he told her it was best just to leave it at that. Lady Seaforth, however, would not drop the subject and Kenneth was goaded into declaring that his master was with a beautiful French courtesan in her chamber. Stung by anger and by her humiliation in front of her friends, she accused Kenneth of lying and practising witchcraft. He was dragged away by two of the servants at Lady Seaforth's command to be tried for witchcraft. The next day, he was given a summary trial and found guilty. But not before he was able to forecast the decline and fall of the Seaforth family in the not too distant future. He affirmed with relish that the final Earl in direct line would have four sons but he would outlive them all. The line would die out, which came true in the early nineteenth century."

"What was his punishment?" asked Johnnie.

"The Countess had him put upside-down in a barrel of burning tar. A horrible death. Literally, a sticky end. There's a final twist too. Lord Seaforth had returned to Scotland that day landing further south. On the way, when he was riding home, someone told him of the trial. He rode like a bat out of hell to stop the execution, but arrived too late."

"So, Kenneth's gifts were a double-edged sword, eh?" said Johnnie "They made him famous, but killed him in the end."

Murdo remarked to Dolligan that Kenneth had predicted the Highland Clearances in the 19th century too.

"Yes. Have you heard of them, Johnnie?"

"I've read about them. The aristocratic landlords threw their poor tenants off their crofts and put sheep on the land instead because it made them more money."

"Och aye, it was a great scandal. They were terrible times. People had nowhere to go and a great many starved to death. That's why so many emigrated to North America." Dolligan's expression darkened.

His lips tightened. "The flower of the Scottish people died or left. My great grandfather Iain and his family were thrown off their croft in Great Bernera, a very small island a few miles from here. It's only 200 yards off the coast of Lewis. They built a bridge to it a few years ago but there was no connection in those days. Himself, his wife and son Donald put their few essential possessions in a rowing boat, rowed down Loch Roag and landed in Callanish. The local blacksmith, James Nicholson, took them in. The blacksmith was usually the richest working-class man in any village, although "rich" is a bit of an exaggeration. It's all relative. Everyone needed metal things made and of course, shoes for horses and ponies. The smithy was the social centre for the old men. Particularly in the winter. The forge is always very warm and they used to gather there for a good natter. Having no children, he took on Donald as an apprentice and when James, who was a widower, died about fifteen years later, James left him the blacksmith's forge and the house. So.........that's how the Macleod family ended up in Callanish."

"What he didn't tell you is that the family were known in the village as the "Fighting Macleods." Donald and his wife used to fight like cat and dog. They both had really fiery tempers. Every so often, Donald would throw his wife Flora out of the house. She'd stay with friends at the other end of the village for a few days, then come back when he'd cooled down."

Catriona's features clenched. "Murdo, that gives people the totally wrong impression about them." she protested. "They were well respected. He was a great blacksmith."

Murdo grinned mischievously, holding his palms innocently in the air. "I agree. I'm only trying to give a more rounded picture. It also explains that central thread that runs through our family's tradition. Stubbornness and tenacity. With a wee dash of aggression thrown in. Be honest, Catriona, Mum had all three. In spades."

"I don't know about that, Murdo............," she said tentatively, with a worried look, not sure where the conversation was leading.

"She was a great mother. Very warm, tough, and capable too. But, let's face it, there was a flip side to these qualities."

"How d'you mean?"

"Catriona, be honest. She was very aggressive and pushy. She was the type of woman who spends her whole life demanding to see the manager."

Dolligan gave a crooked, ironic smile, remembering his sister. "That's a nice way of putting it."

Warming to his theme, Murdo continued with a sparkle in his eye. "She probably did that when she stood at the Pearly Gates as well. "I know you're Saint Peter, but I want to talk to someone more senior,"" mimicked Murdo impishly.

Catriona was not impressed with the conversation and her thunderous expression reflected this. "Show a bit of respect, Murdo," she reproved loudly.

Although he didn't like her faults, Calum had still loved his grannie a lot. She was a bit of a Jekyll and Hyde and the good side of her was warm and loving. Particularly with her kids and grandkids. So, trying to act as the peacemaker, he quickly interposed, "She was very generous and hard-working and made great marags. She said the secret was to put plenty onions in. She often sent me off to the slaughter-house just up the road on Westview Terrace for blood, which was free. She would give me an empty one of those shiny metal tins they used to put milk in. Held about two pints. She'd put a big pile of salt in the bottom. At the slaughter-house, they would sit me down in a little bare reception room, and take away the tin. Then, a couple of minutes later they'd come back with it filled with warm sheep's blood. The salt stopped it going off."

Johnnie, screwed up his face with distaste. "That's a nasty job. Didn't it bother you?"

"Nah. Not really. Except……well, once. They played a nasty trick on me. Took me into the abattoir itself. It was like Hell itself in there. Animals being trussed up and killed all over the place. The smell of hot blood and dead flesh was literally diabolical. They slit a sheep's throat in front of me and held the tin under its neck. I don't know to this day why they did it. I was only about ten. We had sausages for dinner that day and Grannie couldn't understand why I wouldn't eat them."

Catriona was horrified. "You never told me this before!"

"I didn't tell Grannie, either. She'd have stormed up to the slaughter-house."

"……demanding to see the manager," laughed Murdo.

Before Catriona could rebuke Murdo again, Johnnie jumped in. "She sounds a fascinating woman. Tell me about her, Catriona."

"She was. She died in 1958, a year after Dad. She was brought up in this house here with three brothers, Norman and Alan (the two that were killed in the First World War) and Dolligan plus an older sister, Auntie Annie, who died a few years ago. She married my father and had three sons and three daughters. Alina's the eldest followed by me, Iain, Murdo, Donald and Kirsty, Kirsty's married with three boys and lives in Carloway, eight miles up the coast from Callanish. They're a lovely family and although they've never been well-off, Kirsty's a great mother, works hard and laughs a lot. I've never known anyone with such a happy nature. Nothing ever seems to get her down. Either that, or she hides it well. We see her and the family quite a lot. Her husband's a crofter with sheep."

"What was your mother's nickname?"

"Bean a bèicear (ben a vay-kyar]. In other words, the baker's wife."

Alina never married and lives on Macaulay Road. Very generous and loves kids. Works in one of the mills. Iain spent most of the Second World War in a prisoner of war camp in Germany. He was a dispatch rider. As you can see we're not a lucky family when it comes to wars! But, Iain - or Bunny as he's always known - has that Macleod grit. He escaped twice but got recaptured. I reckon if he'd done it again, they'd have sent him to Colditz. When his POW camp was liberated in early 1945, he begged to go back into action to help in the final assault on Germany to get his own back on the Gerries after all those years. He emigrated to Toronto about five years ago, married a nurse and works on one of the Great Lakes. They've three young children as well. Then there's my youngest brother, Donald - or Dollan to give him his nickname."

"Dollan is always called the black sheep," explained Murdo "although it's not fair on him."

"Why's that?" asked Johnnie.

"Bunny was always my mother's favourite. Hard working and reliable. Foreman at Dugie's the Butchers. Mum treated him like a prince. Put him on a pedestal. Dollan on the other hand was always in hot water, a bit of a rebel. Just teenage things really, fighting and drinking. He wasn't very reliable and lost jobs because of it. So my mother had a down on him and treated him as a rogue. He got fed up in the end and left the island in 1949. Since he left, he's never contacted home once. Ever. Not even a letter. He was always a free spirit with a strong, forceful personality – and a wee bit wild."

Murdo grinned nostalgically as he thought of Dollan's harum-scarum exploits as a youth. "He knows how to look after himself in a fight and takes no cheek from anyone. No-one knew exactly where he was but every so often he would turn up unannounced at Catriona and Harry's in Kilmarnock for a visit. Catriona was his favourite sister and like everyone else, he respected Harry. He's apparently done well enough for himself and when he last saw Catriona he had his own house in West Ham in London and lives with a local girl. He's a foreman in a factory making electrical motors. Looks like being a foreman runs in our family. My mother would have made a great foreman too! Anyway, that's it - you've heard the family history now."

"There's a spooky tale about Dollan as well," said Catriona. He told me once that he'd just gone to bed one night, when his father's ghost appeared at the foot of the bed. He assured me it definitely wasn't a dream. He was wide awake. His father asked him why he'd never kept in touch and what he'd done with his life. Was he happy now?"

She looked at Johnnie. "Dollan later found out that this was the night Alec died. He had obviously come to see his long-lost son to set the record straight."

Everyone was silent for a short spell, thinking about the sadness and poignancy of it all. Johnnie broke the short silence. "What about your father's family, Murdo?"

"They came from Bayble, a village in Point, a small peninsula just east of Stornoway. Its correct name is The Eye Peninsula. My mother fell out with Alec's family big-time just after the wedding and she never took us to see my father's relatives. She said they weren't a very close family but......who knows how true that is. I think she manoeuvred it that way to freeze out Dad's family. Maybe I'm being unfair, I don't know"

Johnnie changed the subject. "Incidentally, I've just found out an interesting fact about the islands which surprised me. Particularly, since no-one on the island seems to know anything about it, either. Apparently, Mount Hekla in Iceland erupted in a big way in the twelfth century B.C. The effect on the whole of Scotland, including Lewis, was catastrophic. The population of Scotland was reduced by more than 90 percent by the eruption, spewing 12 cubic kilometres of volcanic dust into the atmosphere. This massive dust-cloud blocked most of the sunlight and changed the climate for many years to come. It was like a nuclear winter. The temperature dropped like a stone."

"Crikey!", exclaimed Murdo. "I didn't know that."

"Yes." Johnnie affirmed. "Suddenly, farming became almost impossible, The remaining people moved to the coasts to scratch a living. Before the eruption, the island's climate was much warmer and drier. Farming had been fairly easy. There were a lot more trees but many of them died off. This and the huge increase in rainfall led to the creation of water-saturated peat-bogs. It was an environmental disaster. What's more, if all this wasn't enough, the chaos caused armed conflict to break out and settlements became fortified, as people fought for habitable land. A war of survival. The experts are not exactly sure when life became normal again but it must have been some time."

"Well, I'm blowed," said Dolligan, nearly dropping his pipe. "I've never heard this before. Can't believe no-one knows about it here. It's pretty bad when a Norwegian has to be the one to tell us locals about our own history. Have any books been written about it?"

"Not yet. That's why nobody knows about it."

Calum knew exactly what that answer meant. The others didn't. They made no comment, putting it down to just another example of Johnnie's eccentricity.

Johnny brought up the Stones. "I've also been reading about the famous Callanish standing stones. I could see them as we climbed the hill. I want to go and see them before we go - if that's alright with you, Catriona."

"Aye", said Murdo. "They're a bit like Stonehenge, but not quite as grand. Apparently they were built around 3,000 BC. Before the Pyramids. No-one knows who put them there and why. At that time, the locals were supposed to be savages without the technology to move the stones, let alone erect them. There are a few local myths about this. The commonest one is that they were put up by people from somewhere very far away who wore feathered robes. Anyway, who knows." Murdo stared at the fire pensively.

Johnnie again changed the subject. "I've got another fascinating bit of information for you. It's nothing to do with Lewis whatsoever. Did you know that there are lots of spooky, uncanny similarities about the deaths of Presidents Lincoln and Kennedy?"

He counted out the points on his fingertips.

"Lincoln was elected to the House of Representatives in 1846, Kennedy in 1946. Lincoln was the losing candidate for his party's vice-presidential nomination in 1856, Kennedy in 1956. Lincoln was elected president in 1860, Kennedy in 1960. Both their Vice Presidents and successors were called Johnson, who were born in 1808 and 1908. The man defeated by Lincoln in the presidential election, Stephen Douglas, was born in 1813. Kennedy beat Richard Nixon who was born in 1913. Kennedy's secretary was called Lincoln. Both were elected with less than 50% of the vote. After shooting Lincoln, Booth ran from a theatre and was apprehended, shot and killed in a warehouse; Oswald ran from a warehouse and was apprehended in a theatre, a cinema theatre that is………"

"Heavens…….." gasped Calum.

Johnnie smiled and held his hand up. "Hang on. I haven't finished yet. Lincoln was shot in Ford's Theatre. Kennedy was shot in a Ford car, a Ford Lincoln. Both presidents had four children, and one of their sons died during their presidency. Both had been captains of ships in their private lives, Lincoln of a river boat, and Kennedy of a torpedo boat during the Second World War. Both presidents were shot in the head on a Friday sitting beside their wives. Both were accompanied by another couple and the male member of that couple was wounded by the assassin. Lincoln sat in box number 7 at Ford's Theater; Kennedy sat in car number 7 in the motorcade. Both assassins' full names, John Wilkes Booth and Lee Harvey Oswald, had three words, a total of 15 letters each. Both assassins were killed before being tried, They both committed the murders in the building where they worked (Booth was an actor who sometimes performed in Ford's Theatre). Both assassins were from the South in their mid-20s, born in 1838 and 1939…..and both their bodyguards were called William, who died at exactly the same age to the month."

"That's really weird, isn't it?" wondered Murdo.

Dolligan looked up at the ceiling. "Well, at least it shows the Good Lord has a sense of humour."

There was a knock on the door and Mairi rose from her seat. "Come in, Toffee." She'd seen him pass the window.

In came a tall, well-built middle-aged man in a heavy, dark blue woollen pullover with a blue plaid cloth cap on his grey, curly head. "I saw Catriona's car outside so I thought I'd say hello. Hope I'm not interrupting anything."

Catriona stood up and walked towards him with a hug. "Och, no. Not at all, Toffee. We've finished dinner. Sit down and have a cup of tea."

He sat down at the table and helped himself from the pot, refusing any food. "We've only just finished eating ourselves. How are you, Catriona?"

"Glè mhath," (glay-vah) she replied favourably. "Have you met Johnnie Samhach? Johnnie Quiet. He's over from Norway for a while."

The two men shook hands and smiled cordially.

"Taking a break from the weaving for a wee bit?" asked Dolligan. Toffee nodded. Dolligan pointed his pipe at the new arrival. "Johnnie, this fella's a Harris tweed weaver as well as a crofter. Calum says you're really interested in how it all works."

Taking Dolligan's cue, Toffee explained that to qualify as real Harris tweed, and get the official "Orb" stamp, the cloth must be woven by Lewis or Harris crofters at home on non-motorised looms. They're operated by hands and feet. The mills in Stornoway spin the wool and deliver the bobbins of raw spun yarn to the crofters to weave into lengths of tweed according to their pattern instructions.

"Where do you keep the loom?"

"In a big shed next to the house. I get my wool from Sticky's mill. God knows where the family got that weird nickname. Their proper name's Mackenzie." He grinned as he took a draw on his roll-your-own cigarette. "You probably find all these Lewis nicknames really strange but it's just part of our culture, as you've probably worked out by now. I got mine because I loved toffee as a kid. Still do. Each tweed has a standard length and width and we get paid per tweed. Within reason, we can work whatever hours we want, so it's not like being in a factory. Me and my son, Coinneach......Kenneth to you....we each do a six hour shift, four days a week. Can't do it full-time, because we've got to work on the croft ……….. and look after the sheep, of course."

"Ah, so you have sheep too, eh? How many do you have?"

Toffee smiled and Dolligan winked at Johnnie.

"You never ask a crofter that question."

Seeing Johnnie's confused expression, Dolligan went on. "Och well. You see. It's like this. They get government grants for each sheep............so sometimes, they own more than you might imagine, if you see what I mean. I'll let you work it out for yourself. However, I'm quite sure Toffee doesn't do anything he shouldn't. Do you now?" Toffee's face was a picture of wide-eyed innocence.

Mairi put some more peats on the fire, took the ashpan out gingerly from underneath and emptied it outside. "You have to be very careful carrying peat ash, Johnnie. It's really light. The dust is very, very fine, and much lighter than coal ash. So it's dead easy to spill."

Toffee coughed, sucked on his cigarette and took up the story again, "When we finish the tweeds, they pick them up and take them back to the mill in Stornoway. They then finish the job. They wash it because it's a very oily wool and do other things to give it a nicer finish. It's also checked very closely for flaws. That's what Catriona's sister, Alina does. She's called a darner. She examines it on a wooden roller and if she finds a very minor fault, she darns it with a needle and thread. If it can't be repaired properly, she rejects it and a section gets cut out."

"What's the money like?"

"Nothing special, but it keeps the wolf from the door. The sheep and the croft aren't nearly enough to live on on their own."

"Is it reliable?"

"Aye. At the moment, anyway," he conceded, closing his tobacco tin. "This new lightweight tweed's been a great success and it's really revived the sales which were beginning to wilt a bit. It's become a fashion item, particularly in England and America." He squashed out his cigarette in the ashtray. "But the trade's really at the mercy of fashion. I'm worried if there's a bad downturn, some of the mills might close and won't be around to take advantage when things swing back in their favour." He stood up, drained the last of his tea and stretched. "Anyway, it's time I wasn't here. I've got some more work to do. Good to see all you Stornowegians again. Drive carefully back to the big city............ and don't forget your poor country cousins, scratching a living out here in the sticks."

Murdo snorted loudly and grinned. "Mach a seo! Get away with you, Toffee! You've got more money than any of us. Blinking farmers and crofters! They're always claiming poverty."

Toffee smiled back and shrugged. When he had gone, Johnnie rose from his chair and stretched his arms. "I think I'll have a walk up to the stones."

"I'll come with you," offered Calum.

"No, you've probably seen them plenty times before."

Calum could tell by his manner Johnnie wanted to go on his own, so he dropped the idea.

"See you later."

Just before he left, Johnnie took Calum to one side and spoke in a quiet tone. "Just a word of warning, Calum. Be careful what you say to people about me. If too much gets around, it could lead to trouble. I might have to leave the island earlier than intended. Don't mention my…umm…..eccentricities. Like second sight. Be careful what you give away. Learn to be discreet. It'll serve you well in life." Calum nodded sheepishly, red-faced with embarrassment. He didn't like displeasing Johnnie.

"Remember that wisdom is more important than knowledge."

"How d'you mean?"

"Knowledge is knowing that a tomato is a fruit. Wisdom is knowing not to put it in a fruit salad."

When Johnnie started to walk up the road towards the stones, the wind was starting to rise and a persistent drizzle was falling. Since it was after four o'clock, twilight was setting in. This far north, the days are still short in early March. As he reached the small hill, he saw the megaliths, set in the shape of a cross with a circle of stones at the junction. He knew a lot more about them than he had let on to the family. An awful lot more than the family themselves did in fact.

Set on a hill overlooking Loch Roag, a sea loch, an inlet cutting into the rocky shore, they were a magnificent achievement in their time, with the largest over 15 feet high and weighing nearly six tons. The Grand Avenue is 270 feet long. The stones themselves are not as stylishly fashioned as Stonehenge. They're thinner. More jagged and uneven. Like a row of old witches' teeth.

True to form, the weather had taken a capricious turn for the worse. The chinks of blue from earlier had gone. Instead, brooding clouds of varying shades of dark grey boiled and churned angrily in the darkening sky. Icy rain was sheeting in over the loch, carried on a strong, biting wind. The wind scudded shivering ripples across the loch. On a mild day, the view was beautiful. However, on a day like this with the elements sourly roaring their incontinent fury, it was positively atmospheric. Johnnie, however, was unaffected by this. He seemed transfixed by the stones. Removing a medallion-like object which hung on a chain round his neck, he put it in the palm of his left hand and placed both hands on one of the larger stones, talking to himself animatedly. The rain plastered his sparse blond hair to his brow. The wind immediately reached a crescendo, a screaming storm force. Almost like a mini-tornado. Lightning forked from the sky.

Suddenly, there was no sign of Johnnie at all. He had literally disappeared into thin air.

Chapter 4

"Where've you been, Johnnie? You've been away for over two hours." It was Murdo coming towards the stone circle with Calum. "It's nearly seven. We were a bit worried with the wild weather setting in and we could see flashing lights on the hill. Must have been lightning – but we didn't hear any thunder, which is strange."

Avoiding Calum's eyes, Johnnie replied calmly, "It's easy to mistake the time when you're enjoying yourself."

The smell of wet grass and heather filled the air. Calum could see a wild sparkle in Johnnie's eye that belied his otherwise stolid manner. What's more, Johnnie should have been drenched in the sheeting rain, but he – and his clothes – were remarkably dry. Weird, thought Calum.

When they got back to Dolligan's, Mairi was beaming. "The wanderer returns! Sit yourselves down. I've made some scones on the griddle over the fire. We'll have them with a cup of tea." They all sat round the table. Abjuring his usual water-drinking habits out of politeness, Johnnie instead accepted a cup of steaming black tea, and was passed a plate of warm, flat, wedge-shaped, floury griddle scones. After he'd taken one, Mairi pointed to a plate of what looked like cottage cheese in a patty shape. "It's home-made crowdie. It's like cottage cheese but drier. Slightly sour. Some people like it on a scone on its own, but others prefer it mixed with cream. It's moister and richer in flavour that way." Johnnie tried it on its own on a scone and nodded sagely in appreciation. "Have a chocolate biscuit as well." But Johnnie declined.

"He's a very small eater, Mairi," said Catriona by way of excuse.

So after a few hours they all set off back to Stornoway. The journey was uneventful, although the rain and wind lashed the car windows with a surly malevolence as if annoyed it couldn't get at them. Calum was quiet, though. Unsettled and perplexed. Johnnie didn't speak once on the journey, his eyes glued to the window all the way.

The following evening, Calum and Johnnie were sitting on their own in front of the fire in the living room, as Catriona did the ironing in the kitchen.

"What happened at the stones yesterday?"

"I had to be somewhere else for a while. I'll tell you about it when the time's right," Johnnie said abstractedly, not raising his eyes from his anthropology book.

Calum was often frustrated by Johnnie's secretiveness. "You're always saying something like that." He protested huffily. "I don't understand why."

"There's a right time for everything, Calum. Learn patience. Don't worry, everything will be revealed to you in good time."

When early summer came, and the football season started (in the Hebrides, soccer is played in summer, not winter, because of the climate), Johnnie would go to the United Rovers matches and support Calum from the sidelines, but at a slight distance. They were the best junior team on the island and Calum was an inside forward. He'd never be good enough to play for Kilmarnock for sure, or even Ross County, but he enjoyed it. One Friday evening, some weeks after the visit to Callanish, Murdo called round at about 7pm and spoke to Johnnie.

"Why don't you come out with me for a drink tonight? There are some interesting characters in the bars I go to."

Johnnie shook his head. He wasn't fond of crowds. He liked to keep a low profile.

Catriona grinned. "Can you imagine, Johnnie? For a small town with only 6,000 people, Stornoway's got at least twenty bars and pubs!" adding disapprovingly, "It gets pretty wild down in town on a Friday and Saturday night. Fights and drunks all over the place and what not."

"That's a bit of an exaggeration, Catriona. Besides, we're only going to The Star Inn. It's an older man's pub. The only trouble they get down there is people complaining about rheumatism or losing their false teeth. Don't worry, I'll look after him."

"Actually, on second thoughts, it'll probably do you good to have a night out for a change," said Catriona changing her mind. After a few minutes persuasion by Murdo, Johnnie went along with the idea against his better judgement.

On the way down the road, Murdo opened the conversation.

"I wanted a word with you on your own, anyway. I work out things quite fast. I've been watching very closely and I've made a decision about you." Johnnie eyed him with wary interest.

"I believe you're from somewhere very different to Norway. I don't know exactly where that is or why you're here but I think it's something to do with Calum. Helping him in some important way. You've had a fantastically positive influence on him. You're like a father and Catriona's spirits have been transformed too." Johnnie looked straight ahead without expression or comment, as Murdo continued.

"It's also obvious you're a very honourable and admirable man. I can sense it's for Calum's good, so I'm not going to tell anyone of my suspicions and I'm not going to interfere. I've made the decision I'm going to trust you. Can you tell me a bit more?"

"Your intuition is spot on, Murdo. But, no. Only Calum will be told the full story of who I am and why I'm here……and not quite yet. It's essential no-one else knows. Trust me, my mission is very serious and important. It won't just help Calum, either."

"OK, I believe you. I'll go along with that. I won't bring it up again."

"Thank you, Murdo." Johnnie looked genuinely relieved.

After a short gap, Johnnie changed the subject. "Why are you so sarcastic and cynical about life?"

Murdo ruminated for a few moments and sighed. "Because at heart, I suppose I'm just a sentimental utopian. I lost faith in the Free Church early on and I thought socialism was the answer. But it turns out it's a fraud. A sort of counterfeit Christianity. All the egalitarian bits without the difficult spiritual dilemmas and obligations. A religion without a soul. Just when I thought I'd discovered the meaning of life, they changed it," Murdo quipped with a weak smile. "So, I'm left with nothing. The world's still full of evil and getting worse. It all seems pointless.........and what's God doing about it, if He's there at all? Nothing. I hope he's got a bloody good excuse."

Johnnie looked slightly exasperated and shrugged.

"I don't know for sure why God lets evil continue either. As I said before, it's probably because you can't have good without evil. There's no day without night. You can't just expect the answer to be dead simple anyway, wrapped up in a neat box with a pretty red bow. Are you just going to mope around like a spoiled child because the cosmos is unfathomable and the human race doesn't live up to your utopian ideals? You said the other day you're a realist but if you were, you'd recognise that people seem to have been designed with flaws. Why can't you see there's a cosmic dimension to everyone's lives? Humans are spiritual beings. As an American psychic once said, "You're not a human being having a spiritual experience. You're a spiritual being having a human experience."

You're also an intelligent man. Don't let the faults of the messengers put you off the message. If the Free Church offends your delicate sensibilities, find another Christian church or other set of metaphysical beliefs that fit your ideas better. For goodness sake, rise out of your spiritual lethargy. Otherwise, your spirit will wither and dry up for good. Like a ball of brushwood blowing in the wind in the Kansas dust-bowl."

Murdo was a little taken aback by Johnnie's candid, out-spoken comments. But, underneath, he knew they were fair.

"You need to replace that void in your soul with belief in something, Murdo. And never, ever give up on optimism. It always sounds smart and mature to be cynical all the time about life. It's not. It's an admission of defeat. A pessimist lives his life in permanent winter. Get some sun on your soul. Unless you're one of the lucky ones, you'll only get your threescore and ten in this life."

Murdo looked away at the passing traffic without comment. He wasn't angry at all. He just didn't enjoy facing the truth.

Johnnie summed it up. "Time wasted is time lost."

After a half-hour walk down Macaulay Road, Bayhead and Cromwell Street – the main street in Stornoway - they came to the harbour, then turned right on to South Beach. Murdo inhaled the salty, fishy breeze, which he loved. Some seagulls were making quite a din next to the harbour wall, fighting over a dead, half-squashed herring in a discarded, broken fish box. Two hundred yards on the right they arrived at The Star Inn, a white-washed detached building that could have been mistaken for a medium-size house but for the large name-sign on the wall. Leading the way, Murdo opened the door and walked to the bar. The warmth hit them straightaway.

"Evenin', Pat," he said to the landlord. The bar was full and there was a babble of different conversations. All men, predominantly middle-aged or old. Pipe and cigarette smoke mixed with the slight smell of whisky and beer.

Johnnie followed gingerly with a wary, alert expression. He looked nervous. As if he was entering a lion's den. The bar was not big, much longer sideways than front-ways. There were two young barmen with open-necked white shirts. In the middle, pulling a pint was Pat Foley, the landlord, about five foot nine, stocky and dressed in an old-fashioned, greeny-brown patterned cotton shirt, with a clashing blue tie. His trousers were green above dark brown, well-polished shoes.

However, Pat's most striking feature was that he was the spitting image of Nikita Krushchev, the Russian leader. A rotund, florid face with a bulbous nose, beneath a bald head. People started nicknaming him Krushchev at first when he arrived from Glasgow but because he took such great exception to it, only a few people persisted. If he had been unpopular, his protestations would have gone unheeded, but his generous, jolly manner made him almost universally liked. Pat came from a very impoverished Irish Catholic background in Glasgow and like most Glaswegians had a ready wit. He often explained they were so poor that his mother used to buy all their clothes second hand from the Army and Navy Stores. He said it wasn't much fun going to school dressed as a Japanese admiral.

"A pint of heavy for me….. and you?" said Murdo glancing at Johnnie, who opted for an orange juice. Seeing a group of three men at a large table in the left hand corner, playing dominoes, Murdo turned his head.

"Hiya, lads. Mind if we join you?"

"No. Join the ceilidh, Prof," said Kenny Morrison, the old man with the wrinkled face who had been there when Calum fell into the river. Contrary to what mainland people think, a ceilidh is simply a get-together in someone's house or anywhere else for that matter. It <u>can</u> also mean an organised dance but that's not its original meaning.

Murdo did all the introductions. The first of the other two men was Angus Maciver, a tall, slim man of 28, dressed up in a very smart dark blue suit, white shirt and blue and red diagonally-striped tie. Always known as "Guga," Gaelic for gannet, Angus liked to dress up on Friday and Saturday nights because he went to the dance after closing time. He was popular with the ladies and had a roving eye. Guga is a culinary delicacy to a small number of islanders but most of the others wouldn't go near it with a barge-pole. An acquired taste, perhaps – to be generous.

The guga are Northern gannets, also called solan geese, and they live on the side of steep cliffs on an island off the Northern coast of Lewis. Every summer, the local people capture them with long poles with nooses attached and salt them, which heightens the naturally salty taste caused by the birds' diet of sea-fish. They also have an oily, fatty flavour – and a very strong, distinctive aroma. Angus was given one to taste when he was a young lad and his disgusted reaction generated his nickname. On being told it tasted half-way between steak and mackerel, he pronounced with a grimace, "More like skunk and walrus."

The other man was Jimmy Buchanan, a tall, well-built Glaswegian in his mid-fifties. Jimmy was more comfortably dressed in a royal blue polo shirt, dark blue V-neck pullover, smart charcoal-grey slacks and black shoes. He was a pipe smoker and liked his whisky. "Bell's" was his label, which he called "Ding Dong." Many people thought he looked like an older version of Billy McNeil, the Scottish footballer. Guga and Jimmy worked together at the fishmeal factory near the harbour, where Jimmy was the foreman.

"Aye, Kenny's telt us a' aboot ye, Johnnie Quiet," Jimmy said in his Glasgow brogue. "Ye're a brave man. Well done. Kenny says ye're a bit o' a seer too."

"Oh, no!" thought Johnnie, "here we go again."

However, seeing Johnnie's discomfiture, Murdo jumped in quickly, "No, no," he said with a disdainful look. "Total load of rubbish! Just the rumour factory exaggerating things. Bunch of bloody, clacking old women." Everyone seemed to accept this.

"You're Norwegian, I hear," said Guga. Johnnie nodded warily, taking a parsimonious sip of his orange juice and trying to look inconspicuous. He wished he was somewhere else. Anywhere but here.

Changing the subject, Murdo nodded towards a drunk-looking man at the bar. "I see Dosan's well-oiled already." Dosan (<u>Doss</u>-an) was a short, slightly-built man in his late thirties, but he looked ten years older, with a sharp-cornered face, a weathered tan and a thatch of extremely thick, shiny, wavy black hair. One thing certain, he'd never go bald. His attire was scruffy. He'd come straight from work.

"The black wellies, that's his trade-mark," said Guga. "Wears them all the time. He'd need a bloody operation to get them off. A welly-ectomy. The tops are always turned down too."

"Aye, for that extra bit of elegance," suggested Kenny.

"That's a funny name..........Dosan," said Johnnie. "Is it a nickname?"

"Yeah, Gaelic," said Guga, who was fluent. "It means the hair on the front of the head, the fringe. You'll find out later why it's his nickname," he added mysteriously. "He's a poor truachan. Poor soul," he added for Johnnie's benefit. "His mother died about ten years ago. He never got over it. Lives with his father in Laxdale a few miles outside town, about a mile down the road from my house. They live in a caravan."

"Is he a ceard, then?" asked Jimmy.

"No, not everyone that lives in a caravan's a tinker, you know."

The tinkers - or ceards in Gaelic [pronounced kyards, "c" is always hard in Gaelic] - have been on the island for some time. Originally, they were gypsies who made a living sharpening scissors and knives as well as mending and selling pans. In the modern age, however, this trade is in negligible demand and they are looked down on by many of the other locals as unreliable ne'er-do-wells.

"Naw, I know that. Most of the tinkers are ok, anyway," said Murdo. "Just a bit rough and ready, that's all."

"Aye," said Jimmy, a left-wing Red Clydesider, raising his glass. Paraphrasing Rabbie Burns, he added, "A man's a man for a' that. We're a' Jock Tamson's bairns." Kenny raised his eyes to the ceiling.

Guga winked at Johnnie. "Aye, that's right. Even you bloody marauding Vikings," he said good-naturedly. Although they swore more colourfully normally, Murdo's pals left out the f's and c's in his company in deference to his being a schoolteacher, a very well-respected profession in Lewis. Education is prized by nearly every Lewis parent, from labourer to lawyer. If they only knew, swear-words would not have bothered Murdo at all. He'd heard a lot worse as a student in the Marischal Bar, and his other drinking haunts in Aberdeen.

Overhearing the conversation, Pat the landlord leant over the bar. "I don't care if you are a Viking," he grinned, "get that bloody axe oot o' the dartboard!"

The whole table erupted in laughter, even Johnnie. He was beginning to enjoy the evening despite himself.

"Anyway, ye were tellin' him a' aboot Dosan," said Jimmy, taking a long puff on his pipe..

"Aye," remembered Guga, "he works for the county council as a labourer on the roads. Supposed to be a very good worker, but every weekend, he's permanently drunk from Friday night at 6 till closing time on Saturday night. Totally blootered. Oblivion. However, his dad makes sure Dosan gives him his food-money on pay-day. He goes out and buys five big steaks from Charlie Barley's and makes Dosan a huge fried steak and onion sandwich for his dinner-break at work every day. And I mean huge. Like a cow's arse hangin' out of a loaf."

By nine o'clock, Dosan was very drunk. A sociable enough man during the week, but in a world of his own all weekend. He was practically unable to speak beyond a mumble. A harmless, non-violent drunk but not much company for anyone either. A solitary tippler by necessity, if not by choice. His head was drooping down nearly on to the bar with his copious, luxuriant curls bobbing and dangling down in ringlets.

"Now, that's why he's called Dosan," winked Guga. "He does it all the time."

Ten minutes later, Dosan got off his seat and tottered out the door.

"He'll be off to the public bar in the "Crown." At closing time he'll stagger along to the bus stop opposite the Rendezvous Café," went on Guga "I don't understand it. He's totally blootered, but he never misses the last bus. He's not as daft as he looks. Always knows when it reaches Laxdale too. Must be on automatic pilot. I was talking to Iain Macritchie, one of the barmen in the "Crown" public bar, You know, the student that works there in the summer holidays. Comes from Fivepenny in Ness. Now there's a great name for a village, isn't it, Johnnie? Anyway, Iain says people underestimate Dosan. He talks to him early in the evening when he's sober. He really likes him. Although he says he's no intellectual giant, he's an honest, decent man."

"Aye. He's right about the intellectual bit, though," commented Murdo. "I doubt if they talk much about Cartesian Dualism."

"Maybe not - whatever the hell that is - but he says Dosan often borrows a ten-bob note off him just before closing time on a Saturday night. "Have you got a "greenback," Iain?" he always says, tottering on his wellied feet. The uncanny thing is though, Dosan always remembers the loan, and he always pays him back."

"A gentleman, then. Even if not a scholar. As the saying goes."

"It's my round," said Guga. Unlike Kenny, who lived on the old-age pension and had a reputation for meanness, Guga was always generous with his money. "Two pints o' heavy, an orange juice, a Dewar's for Kenny and...." with a wink "....a Ding Dong for Jimmy." Guga brought the drinks from the bar on a tray and sat down again. "Anybody want some crisps, or a hot pie or somethin'?" he added as an afterthought.

Everybody shook their heads.

"I'm very surprised. The food in here's untouched by human hand." Guga looked at Pat with a wicked twinkle in his eye. "Honest. It's absolutely true. The chef's a Glaswegian."

"Who are Rangers playing tomorrow?" Murdo asked Jimmy, a staunch "Gers" supporter, who had just stuck two fingers up to Guga after his last remark.

"They're away tae Hearts. Tough match."

Turning to Pat behind the bar, Murdo asked, "What about Celtic?"

"What would Pat know aboot fitba?" interjected Jimmy. "He's a left-fitter."

"What's that?" queried Johnnie.

"A left-footer," explained Murdo, enunciating the word in an exaggeratedly correct way, dropping the glottal stop. "Slang for a Roman Catholic."

Rangers are, of course, the Protestant team in Glasgow, Celtic the Catholic one. The supporters don't even go to the same bars. The hatred is tribal, a relic of the internal strife and internecine wars between the two halves of Christianity over the centuries. A lot of Catholics from the south of Ireland and Protestants from the north settled in Glasgow in the nineteenth and twentieth centuries, bringing their prejudices with them. As if there wasn't enough prejudice and religious friction in Scotland to go round already.

The irony is if you were a foreigner and shown a photograph of the crowd at a Rangers-Celtic game, you would hardly be able to work out it was a Scottish match. Although both sets of supporters are fanatical Scots, they like to "wind up" the opposing fans. Celtic fans brandish the green, white and orange tricolor of the Republic of Ireland to show off their religious roots. Similarly, a lot of the Rangers fans wave the Union Jack, the British standard, because, unlike the Catholics, the Northern Irish Protestants have always wanted to stay part of the Union, the UK. All very confusing.

However, when Scotland are playing an international match, particularly against England, the Auld Enemy, they all revert to full Scottish mode, carrying the blue and white St Andrew's saltire cross or the red lion on a yellow background, the old Scottish war standard. Not a Union Jack in sight!

Although this rivalry spills over slightly to all parts of Scotland, the violent, nasty hatred is mainly a Glasgow and South-West of Scotland phenomenon. In the 1960's, the northern Western Isles, including Lewis and Harris were ninety-nine percent Protestant and the southern islands in the chain were almost entirely Roman Catholic. A truly weird situation. God obviously enjoys irony. However, there's no real strife. There is still an undercurrent of mild sectarian animosity between the two sides, but it rarely results in violence. Mainly just a very slight mutual suspicion. In Glasgow, Jimmy's joke might well have started a fight, but in Stornoway, said with a smile, it was seen for what it was, merely a leg-pulling remark. Jimmy and Pat were both good pals, anyway, and often went out drinking together on Pat's night off.

"Mind," Kenny piped in, "Celtic ain't hittin' the highspots at the moment, are they, Pat? I doubt if they'll qualify for the European Cup next season."

Pat shook his head ruefully. "Naw. The only way the Celtic players'll get intae Europe next year is if there's another world war."

"Yeah, maybe. But these things can change quick," said Guga philosophically. "It could be different in a few years."

"Johnnie, you need to know that Guga's an incurable optimist," smiled Murdo. "The glass is always half full, never half empty. He still thinks Glenn Miller's just missing."

"By the way, Jimmy," cut in Pat. "I hear the Rangers captain was offered a fabulous deal tae speak at next week's Celtic dinner."

"Aw aye. An' pigs might fly."

"Naw, it's true. They offered him two thousand quid…………an' free private medical expenses for the evenin'."

"Talking about religion," said Murdo. "Johnnie got his first taste of a Wee Free service recently. That Reverend Macarthur's something else, is he not?"

"Aye," said Kenny, "Did you hear about last year when one o' them Happy Clappers on a visit from Alabama suddenly interrupted the sermon, stood up and yelled out "Hallelujah, Lord!" The Reverend gave him a filthy look and shouted "Sit down, you fool! You didn't come here to enjoy yourself!"

"I don't believe a word of it," smiled Guga. "Mind, I've got a better one than that. Macarthur was giving one of his Bible-bashing sermons. Fire and brimstone all over the place. "If you don't repent," he cries, "you'll all go to hell! There will be weeping and wailing and gnashing of teeth." The congregation's shakin' in their boots, then this little old toothless cailleach (<u>cal</u>-yach, old lady) asks in a timid voice, "But Reverend, what if you haven't got any teeth?" He was a bit taken aback at first, then he thought for a second, and shouted out, "False teeth... will be.... provided!"

"Somebody telt me recently," announced Jimmy, "that one o' thae Wee Frees died and was standin' ootside the Pearly Gates. Saint Peter looks up the Book. "Yeah," he says, "ye've led a very religious life, but....I'm afraid I cannae let ye in. Ye're a Wee Free." "What's that got to do wi' it?" says the wee mannie. St Peter frowns at him. "Look, pal," he says, "there's no bloody way we're makin' gruel for one."

Mirth all round.

"Yeah, I've heard about the Pearly Gates," said Murdo. "Apparently, there's a sign there that says, "Welcome to Heaven. Keep your religion to yourself." Co-iudh (co-yoo}, anyway," he went on. "I'm joining this new religious sect that's all the rage. It combines the best bits of Catholic and Jewish traditions and way of life."

Sensing an imminent punch-line, Jimmy asked warily, "Oh, yeah?"

"Yeah. You still have to go to Confession, but you get to bring your lawyer with you."

"I like it," agreed Jimmy, slapping his thigh. "Now, wouldnae that be somethin'? Anyway, let's get back tae the dommies. D'ye want a game as well, Johnnie?"

Johnnie had never played before, but a few minutes' explanation was enough and they started playing again. After the first ten games, Johnnie had won eight, to the astonishment of everyone.

"Bloody hell!" moaned old Kenny with wide-open eyes. "It's uncanny. It's almost as if he knows everybody's hand."

"No, no. Just beginner's luck," protested Johnnie, realising his error. He then started to lose more often, which pleased the others. Although they didn't seem to notice, Murdo could see Johnnie wasn't trying any more.

"Murdo, I hear you broke up with Effie Macdonald," said Guga, placing a winning domino on the table. "Is it true she's an outspoken atheist?"

"Uh-huh. She went to Belfast on holiday last year and somebody asked her if she was a Protestant or a Catholic. When she said she was an atheist, he replied. "OK, fair enough. But is it the God of the Protestants or the God of the Catholics you don't believe in?" She's a bit of a feminist too."

"Aye, I noticed. Did that bother you?"

"Look, mate, feminism only works until the car breaks down. Besides, Effie could be very down on men. She said to me once that God gave men a penis and a brain, but only enough blood supply to run one at a time." Even the men at the next table laughed at that one.

"Come on, be fair, where would we be without them?" asked Kenny.

"In the bloody Garden of Eden with a pint o' heavy an' a fish supper," declared Guga with feeling. Warming to the topic, he suggested, "Look, lads, let's list the ways that men are better than women." The 1960's were never famous for their political correctness. After a short silence while they cogitated, Guga piped up, "Well……..a woman can't become President of the USA."

"Dinnae talk rot, Guga," said Jimmy with a snort.

"It's true. You've got to be over 35."

"So?"

"Where you going to find a woman to admit she's over 35?"

An old man with a green cloth cap and far too much drink on board was staggering slowly past on his way to the toilet. Overhearing the conversation, he stopped and swayed. After a short moment of rumination, he raised one pointed index finger theatrically in the air, as if he had just discovered the secret of the Universe. He let go a hiccup. No doubt inspired by where he was about to go, he said very slowly and deliberately with great solemnity:

"Women can't write their name in the snow with their piss like men can."

"Aye, you're dead right there, pal," said Murdo, quick as a flash, "but they can always add the full stop at the end."

"That old guy's the only man I've ever seen with more wrinkles than our Kenny," teased Guga.

Fortunately, Kenny always had the ability to laugh at himself. He took it in good humour, but still protested.

"They're not wrinkles, Guga, you cheeky bugger. They're laughter lines."

Murdo threw his head back and burst out laughing. "Nothing's _that_ funny, Kenny."

At closing time, after many farewells, Murdo and Johnnie left "The Star Inn" along South Beach and turned on to Cromwell Street past the town hall, where a host of young men and women were milling round and going into the Friday night dance. Outside "The Neptune," a young people's bar on the opposite side of the road. the customers, male and female, were streaming out drunk. Many were raucous but in high spirits, although Johnnie noticed two lads in their early twenties with angry voices, squaring up for a fight at the side of the town hall. Another, with a half bottle of whisky in his back pocket, for sharing with his pals at the dance, was being loudly sick against the newsagent's wall.

"It's like the bloody Wild West," said Murdo.

"All that's missing are the Indians," said Johnnie, throwing in a joke for once.

"No, no, we've got those as well," said Murdo, pointing to the next shop they passed with the device, "Nazir Mohammed, Outfitter" proudly emblazoned above the windows.

Murdo wasn't strictly accurate about the Indians. He was using a bit of poetic licence. There was, though, a thriving and very hard working community of Pakistanis in Stornoway. About thirty perhaps. They started arriving in the early 1950's, selling clothes round the doors and offering credit. Eventually some of them graduated to buying their own shops. There was little friction. The Pakistanis kept themselves to themselves and the locals had a grudging respect for their thrift and strong work ethic. Not exactly integration, though. More like peaceful co-existence.

There was also a small group of Italians in Stornoway. Two families, the Capaldis and the Cabrellis came over just after the Second World War and they later had children and grandchildren. They all integrated completely, the children all had Stornoway accents like the other kids and were very popular. The Capaldis owned the "Rendezvous Café" and the Cabrellis owned the other two cafés in Cromwell Street.

"Let's get a fish supper from the chip shop at the bottom of Church Street," said Murdo. "They're the best in town. I'll buy them. ....of course, I forgot, you don't eat things like that."

So they sauntered home, hands in pockets. To Johnnie's surprise, he had enjoyed himself immensely as Murdo had promised. Carrying on up the main street on the right, past Woolworth's and Cabrelli's

Café opposite, Johnnie pointed towards a figure about thirty yards ahead on the other side of Cromwell Street, staggering past "The Square" restaurant.

"Look, it's Dosan."

Dosan's head was facing mainly downwards with the curls bobbing around like the snakes on the head of Medusa. He was staggering wildly, alternately left and right, foot over foot, moving almost as much sideways as forwards. A dressage drunk. However, he had his destination doggedly in sight. You had to give him full marks for pertinacity, he only had twenty yards to go to the bus stop. Looked like he'd make the last bus yet again. Like a homing pigeon.

Poor, sad Dosan. Life can be hard. As the minister said, "You didn't come here to enjoy yourself."

Chapter 5

Calum and Johnnie were inseparable outside school hours. The following weekend, Calum was kicking a football against the side wall and practising "keepie-uppie," balancing the ball on his feet and head whilst Johnnie was cutting up some wood.

Walking past the house was a brawny - and very drunk – blond man of about six feet three in his mid-twenties who lived across the road. Calum recognised him as Jimmy "Basher." Jimmy wasn't very bright, with an IQ about the same as his shoe-size. Murdo once said that Jimmy hadn't much between his ears. "If you stand close enough to him, you can hear the ocean." A sarcastic teacher once wrote waspishly in his school report. "Jimmy sets himself very low standards and consistently fails to live up to them." When he was sober, Jimmy was not particularly aggressive, merely affecting an air of studied truculence. However, with a few drinks, he had a legendary reputation as a drunken trouble-maker and fighter at the week-end dances. When he was in full flow, he would often wade through a crowd of four or five men, swinging his fists and laying them flat. Hence the nickname. Once, some brave drunk in the Caledonian Bar said to him "You think you're a wit, but you're only half right." Jimmy wasn't fazed at all because he didn't get it. It was only when one of his pals explained it to him that he went up to the man and bopped him on the nose for his temerity.

Unfortunately, Jimmy had drunk quite a few whiskies and beers this day and was spoiling for a fight. Seeing the two of them, he came up the path and approached Johnnie. Swaying slightly and puffing on his cigarette in that exaggerated, over-deliberate, clumsy way that drunks often affect, he slurred:

"So this is Johnnie Quiet, then? Skinny bugger, eh?"

Johnnie ignored him, concentrating on sawing the wood. He gave the impression he could hardly contain his indifference. Moving nearer, with a fiery look in his eye, Jimmy would not be denied. "Don't you bloody-well ignore me!" he said loudly, adding with a contemptuous sneer, "You're not quiet, you're scared. What do you say to that, you yellow bastard?"

At this, Johnnie still kept his eyes on his work but replied evenly "Go away, Jimmy."

But by now the big man was getting incandescent with fury and went to swing a punch. Johnnie looked at Jimmy with the most piercing stare Calum had ever seen and Jimmy staggered back a pace, rubbing his forehead vigorously. Recovering after Johnnie had released him from the grip of his stare, Jimmy wailed "You did something to my mind there! With.....with your eyes." Moving towards Johnnie again, the same thing happened a second time.

"What the hell?...." and wheeling round, he turned aggressively towards Calum. "What are you smirking at?"

Far from smirking, Calum was afraid. Even Johnnie was starting to look worried at the worsening turn of events.

"Jimmy, look over here," Johnnie said to divert him from the boy.

The drunken man turned his head round and was immediately transfixed again by that incredible stare. However, this time, Johnnie didn't let it go. For 10 seconds or so, Jimmy held his head in pain, then fell to the ground. At first, he writhed in agony for another few seconds, then his body slumped like a rag doll.

By this time, Johnnie's usual unflappable manner was cracking. A placid man, unused to personal violence, he kept repeating "Why wouldn't the fool listen? Why wouldn't he listen? I'm not supposed to do things like that! It's not allowed!" It was the first time Calum had ever seen him emotionally distraught.

"He'll be all right when he wakes up," said Calum, shaking.

"No, he won't. He's as dead as a dodo." Quickly recovering his cool, Johnnie told Calum, "Call the ambulance." Putting his right hand on Calum's shoulder he added, "Better not to mention the argument to anyone, ok? It'll only...... complicate things."

The ambulance arrived in about ten minutes. It turned out Jimmy had died of a massive stroke. Because there were no suspicious circumstances or signs of external violence, the police were not called. A well-known drunk had suffered a cerebral haemorrhage during a binge while talking to a neighbour. End of story.

Calum didn't expand on this. To anyone. Ever. Nevertheless, he was disconcerted by the turn of events and that evening when they were on their own in the living room with Catriona working in the kitchen, he expressed his disquiet. "Johnnie," he said, "I'm getting fed up with you telling me nothing when I ask you. You've obviously got very strange powers. I want some answers. First of all, where are you from?"

"Calum, don't you badger me. I'll be the judge of what I reveal to you. And when." Johnnie declared calmly with a severe frown, "Although it's not fashionable in today's world to say it, too much knowledge can do irreparable damage when you're not ready for it. Take my word for it. I'm not prepared to put you into that situation."

Taken aback by the strong, almost aggressive reply, Calum was flustered. "Well at least you could explain why you're here."

"To teach and to learn."

"To teach who...... and learn from who?"

"You. And others like you. There are other, even more important reasons too. Anyway, more of that later. At the right time."

The following afternoon Johnnie was home alone. Catriona was in town shopping and Calum was at football training. He was having a cup of black tea at the kitchen table when the door bell rang. When he opened it, standing there was a very tall, thin man dressed in a white shirt and conservative blue suit and tie. He had a Scandinavian appearance like Johnnie, with an anaemic pallor in his face, and a head shaped like Johnnie's, but he looked about ten years older.

"Hello, Andreas," he said with surprise, "what on earth are you doing here?"

"Aren't you going to invite me in then, Johnnie?" asked Andreas, who had obviously chosen a time when Johnnie was alone.

Johnnie scratched his head absent-mindedly. "Of course, come in. Sorry, I was so surprised to see you, it threw me for a bit," he explained as they walked into the kitchen and sat at the table.

"I'm surprised you're surprised. Did you really think killing that man wouldn't cause big reverberations back home."

"Yes, ok, but I thought it would wait till I got home after my work was done here. Surely, it's really over the top for you to travel here, what with the dangers of exposure and other complications."

The conversation was in English. It is mandatory for them to speak in the local language when they are on a project away from home. Otherwise, sooner or later, there would be a local person within earshot without their knowledge. Johnnie's and Andreas' own language and diction were so strange, so alien, that it would cause suspicion. Not worth the risk.

"The Human Intervention Board sent me to talk to you." Andreas spread his hands on the table as Johnnie listened closely. "You know the rules, Johnnie. If you kill someone deliberately, it's a big crime. If it's unintentional, as it obviously was in your case, it's not an offence. However, it can affect your position as a Teaching Officer if the board think you've been negligent. You're well aware of how sensitive and delicate the intervention project is. You have to be incredibly careful."

He paused as Johnnie protested – vehemently, but very coolly and without anger.

"It's an open and shut case, surely. Both my safety, and more importantly Calum's, were severely in danger."

"Agreed, but you didn't need to kill him. You could have knocked him out for a while."

Johnnie turned his palms upwards and raised his eyebrows. "That's what I was trying to do. I just misjudged the length of time I held him in my grip. And, anyway, you know the mind-stare affects people differently from person to person."

"Yes, fair comment. Nevertheless, some members of the board feel you were negligent. You panicked and lost your temper and that affected your judgement. You're not a human being after all. You've been trained to control destructive emotions. Also, to make things worse, it happened in front of Calum." He shook his head reprovingly, while Johnnie smiled ironically at the unfairness of the charge.

"It's all very easy for you to pontificate theoretically about real-life situations. Things don't always work out by the book. Especially on Earth, They're a very unpredictable species……stubborn, aggressive, tribal and capricious. Often completely irrational."

Andreas leant forward in his seat. "I don't need a lecture from you on the peculiarities of the human race. I've studied them as closely as you have. They're a species in transition. It's our job to lead them on to the next phase in their development. They need to move on to the next stage of their evolution and if we fall down on our job, they won't be able to make that leap."

Johnny shook his head in frustration.

"Look, don't you think I agonised over what happened yesterday? I was devastated."

"I believe you. By the way, about your comments on their terrible weaknesses, I always thought you liked the human race." He smirked cheekily.

"I do, I do. They deserve support. They have great positive qualities – courage, tenacity, and generosity. The best of them are capable of great love and kindness. I was only being a realist about the bad side of their nature. Look, all I'm trying to say is, they're not easy to deal with."

Andreas looked serious again. "To be honest with you, Johnnie, I think the board are being too harsh with you." He pointed his index finger. "Don't tell anyone I said that though. It would drop me right in it. I've been delegated to come here with an unbiased mind and do an impartial report on the situation. Then, when I get home, after a long discussion, we'll all have a vote on your future on the project."

Johnnie clicked his tongue on his teeth, turned his head to the side and looked thoroughly fed up. "I can't believe they might take away my status. This project is my whole life at the moment. I'll be devastated if they take me off it." He looked stricken. "What do you reckon my chances are?"

Andreas wobbled his hands horizontally to indicate it was in the balance. "Not sure. I'll be putting up a strong case for you and I know others will support me. However, we'll have to see." They both stood up and shook hands. "I'll let you know as soon as I know the result."

After Andreas had gone, Johnny wished for a second he was human. He could have had a stiff brandy to raise his spirits. For once, abstemiousness didn't seem such a good thing. Anyway, it wasn't an option. His digestive system couldn't cope with alcohol. It would be poisonous enough to make him fairly ill.

Chapter 6

The weather was changing as summer bloomed and everyone was delighted because Kathy had just come home for the school holidays. She and Calum spent a lot of time outdoors getting the benefit of the warm days and played games indoors on the cold days.

Kathy always loved coming home from school and hated going back to Edinburgh away from the family. One particular morning, a few days after the Jimmy Basher tragedy, Calum and Kathy had planned a picnic together but Kathy felt ill with flu-type symptoms, so she stayed in bed. Her mother gave her a hot drink and an aspirin and looked in on her at about 11.30 am. She could see she was getting worse and felt her forehead.

"She's burning up, the poor wee thing! If she doesn't improve by one o'clock, I'm going to call Dr Maclennan."

By then, however, she was worse, not better. Angus Maclennan, their family doctor, arrived fairly quickly after Calum's call and was led into Kathy's bedroom where her mother was holding a wet, cold cloth on her brow in a vain attempt to cool her down.

"I'm very worried, Angus, she's very hot and feverish. Doesn't seem like ordinary flu."

Standing up so that the doctor could take her seat beside the bed, Catriona couldn't hide her concern. The doctor felt her head, took her temperature and listened to her chest with his stethoscope.

"It's obviously some sort of infection which is causing the fever and you're right. Her temperature's too high."

Frowning, Catriona queried, "Shouldn't she be in hospital, Angus?"

"Not really. There's not much different we can do for her there at this point. She's better at home in bed." Reaching into his surgical bag, he pulled out a bottle of white tablets.

"I'm going to give her some antibiotics and something for the feverishness. That should start to take effect fairly soon. Give her plenty to drink. I've got to make a call in Canada Crescent now but I'll come back in about half an hour to see how she's doing."

By the time he returned, everyone was very distressed as Kathy seemed much worse and she was becoming delirious.

Examining her quickly, Dr Maclennan too was very surprised at her rapid, steep deterioration. He realised if this infection and fever didn't clear very soon indeed, the poor child's life could be in real danger. He gave her more antibiotics and went to the phone to call an ambulance, which arrived in ten minutes. Kathy was put on a stretcher and carried inside with Catriona, Calum and Johnnie anxiously following. With tears in her eyes, Catriona held Kathy's hand. After they arrived at hospital, Kathy was wheeled quickly into the ward. The other three were ushered into the waiting room. A young dark-haired doctor in his thirties with a white coat and stethoscope round his neck explained the treatment.

"We'll give her emergency treatment and once she's stabilised, I'll come and tell you how she's progressing."

Catriona nodded tearfully, wringing her hands. After fifteen anxious minutes, which seemed an age to all three of them, a nurse approached unsmilingly and asked them to follow her into the ward, where Kathy lay in bed motionless with a drip in her arm. The bed was surrounded by a curtain with the doctor at the side of the bed. He explained they had tried desperately to stabilise her and there was nothing more they could do.

"She's got a really severe fever and she's at a crisis point which often happens with fevers. It's like a turning point. She'll either improve soon and get better fairly quickly. Or……she might not make it, I'm afraid." He looked distressed too.

Her mother shot her hand to her mouth and quickly bowed her head as a solemn Calum put his arms round her.

"You can all sit by her bed if you want," said the nurse with a sympathetic look at Catriona.

Sat beside the child's bed, Catriona held Kathy's hand and said a desperate prayer out loud, wiping her eyes at the end.

Meanwhile, Johnnie looked at Catriona with a calm expression. "Let me say my own personal Norwegian prayer for her. You never know, it might help." The others bowed their heads and closed their eyes ready for the prayer as Johnny put his hand on Kathy's brow. Speaking very softly, he intoned his prayer for about a minute, then bowed his own head.

Calum looked at him sadly. "Thanks, Johnnie."

The nurse came back into the room after about another minute. She stood beside the bed, taking the girl's pulse and checking the drip was properly attached. Then she felt Kathy's brow and took her temperature. No words were spoken for what seemed like an age, but was actually only about a minute. With eyebrows raised and a sudden smile on her face, she looked at Catriona.

"Marvellous! Her temperature's dropped nearly two degrees and she even looks better. I can't believe this amount of change could happen so fast."

Meanwhile, on the bed, Kathy stirred. Her eyes flickered and she licked her lips. Catriona clapped her hands ecstatically and Calum grinned broadly. Within ten minutes, she was awake and able to speak, albeit rather weakly. What's more, her fever was receding fast. The doctor arrived with a smile wider than the Mississippi.

"What a relief, Mrs Sutcliffe. I was really worried we'd lose her."

"Thanks for all your help, doctor. You saved her life."

"To be honest, it wasn't really us. There wasn't a lot we <u>could</u> do for her. She was at a crisis point and her own bodily defences did the trick."

For another half-hour, the family continued to sit round the bed excitedly talking to Kathy who was now fully revived, her fever gone, until the nurse arrived again.

"I don't want to break up the party, but I think Kathy needs a bit of quiet now,,,,,,and some sleep. It'll have taken a lot out of her. You must all be whacked too. Go home and come back tomorrow morning. We'll let you know immediately if there are any major developments in the meantime, but everything looks set fair now."

They got a taxi home, much relieved after their ordeal and when they arrived, Catriona was so mentally exhausted she fell asleep in the chair. Meanwhile, Calum and Johnnie went into the kitchen. Calum eyed him with slight suspicion.

"Johnnie, how come she got better almost straight away after you touched her brow? It seems too much of a coincidence to me. You're not a healer as well, are you?"

"Not at all. It had nothing to do with that." His face bore a curious expression. His eyes were grinning but he was managing to smother a smile on his mouth. As if silently encouraging Calum to join up the dots and work out the answer for himself.

"I don't believe you. You're hiding something. I know it. Was it the prayer, then?"

Johnny shook his head, eyes still smiling. "No, no. That was merely a diversion."

"What d'you mean?"

"To get you all to lower your heads, close your eyes and not look at what I was doing. I carry a small phial of special tiny pills with me all the time for emergencies. They're very powerful and fast-acting. They're not a panacea, they can't cure everything. However, they cure a huge range of illnesses and they're particularly effective for fevers and infections. When you weren't looking, I put a pill in her mouth. At the back of her tongue. Easy-peasy!"

Calum gasped. "You old rogue! You're so devious. I bloody knew it was you!"

They eyed each other silently for a second or two. Then, at exactly the same moment, they both burst into manic, raucous laughter. The noise woke up Catriona in the next room. That's great, she thought. Good to see them so happy. A fitting end to a roller coaster day.

After they calmed down, Calum rubbed his chin and looked at Johnnie.

"You do realise that in the space of one week you've taken a life and saved one as well."

"God will forgive me for the first one."

"Why?"

"The deed's not the thing. Intention is everything."

They both nodded and smiled.

Dr. Maclennan popped round to Perceval Road the following afternoon to see how the young girl was. She'd been released from hospital at 1pm. He sat at the kitchen table with Catriona, Calum and Kathy, who was beaming with happiness and relief after her scary experience. She was so obviously completely recovered, he only gave her a cursory examination.

"Well, Kathy, you won't forget that experience for a long time, eh?" He lowered his head slightly. "I feel a bit guilty I didn't send you to hospital earlier........." He scratched his head, "but the final deterioration was so sudden and came on so fast.........."

Catriona jumped in, interrupting him volubly. "Angus, don't be so daft, for goodness sake! Don't you think we understand all that? Don't beat yourself up about it. You were great." Catriona stood up and took a wrapped up box with a bow on it from one of the cupboards. She then presented it to him in his chair, planting a kiss on the top of his head at the same time. "In fact, that's what we think of you, Angus."

Calum could see a hint of wetness in the doctor's eyes, although he was hiding it very well.

"You shouldn't have, Catriona.............." he protested mildly.

"The Corner Shop's only a hundred yards away, so it didn't take me long this morning." She winked. "And we all know how much you love your chocolates."

Suddenly, a sharp cry of pain came from the garden, breaking in on the happy scene. Immediately, Calum jumped up and ran towards the open kitchen door. Johnny was walking quickly towards him holding his right arm, which was gushing blood. His face was a mixture of frustration and pain. "Blast that damned barbed wire! I was mending the post and caught the top of my arm on the blinking thing."

The doctor went over to him and looked closely at the cut, wiping away the copious blood with cotton wool that Catriona had quickly produced.

"It's quite deep and jagged, Johnnie, but it's just as well it's not on the inside of the arm. There's a big artery there and you wouldn't want to sever that. Here, hold that cotton wool over it," he instructed, reaching for his medical bag. Within five minutes he'd cleaned the wound, put surgical spirit on it and wrapped it up very neatly with lint and a bandage.

"That's great. Panic over!" announced Catriona. "Sit down and have a cup of tea, Johnnie. The answer to everything."

Later in the evening at about 7pm, after his last appointment, when Dr Maclennan got home to his large detached house on Goathill Rd, he went straight into his laboratory on the ground floor. His hobby for many years had been examining medical samples, particularly blood, so he had converted his large study to a lab. No expense spared. Haematology in particular fascinated him.

What he hadn't told anyone was that before he left the Sutcliffes' house, he had secreted a blood-sodden piece of cotton wool in his bag. The reason he did this was that he was shocked by the colour of Johnnie's blood. It was virtually pink, not dark red as it should have been. It also seemed a bit thinner than normal. It didn't look right at all.

He took off the jacket of his dark grey three-piece suit and put on his white cotton lab-jacket. He opened his bag, pulled out the badly-stained cotton wool and cut a piece off. When treating Johnnie, he had deliberately over-soaked this particular piece of cotton wool, so it would be easier to get a proper sample from it.

Placing it on a slide, he adjusted the microscope, which was state-of-the-art with very high magnification. In about ten seconds, he suddenly shouted "Bloody hell!" He very rarely swore but he was so astounded by what he'd just seen, he couldn't help it. "This man shouldn't be alive!" The doctor couldn't believe Johnnie's red blood cell count was so low. No-one could survive with blood like this. What's more, the blood cells were the wrong shape. Egg-shaped. He'd never seen blood as strange as this in any animal, let alone a person. He did the experiment again with another piece of the sample. Same result. Maclennan was shell-shocked. He went into the living-room, poured himself a generous dram of single-malt whisky and sank back in his favourite armchair with his arms hanging loosely over the sides and his legs straight out. His hands were shaking and his mind was in a whirl.

Luckily, he had calmed down a little when his wife, Kirsty arrived fifteen minutes later. She'd been visiting a relative in Churchill Drive, not far away. He didn't want to say anything to her yet.

"Angus, I've made us both a cold salmon salad, it's in the fridge. I'll make some new potatoes to go with it."

"Thanks, Curstag." He always called her by the Gaelic version of her name.

Curstag looked round at her husband as she took off her coat and hung it up in the hall. "Are you OK? You look as if you've seen a ghost. Very pale."

Angus smiled inside, thinking to himself "Not as pale as the blood I've just seen!"

"No, I'm fine. Just been a long day. I'm a bit shattered."

First thing in the morning before his first appointment, Angus went straight to the Sutcliffe house. The weather was glorious with a bright sun, no clouds and a warm south wind. "Just thought I'd quickly check up on Johnnie," he told Catriona.

"Sure, Angus. He's out in the garden. What a lovely day."

Angus walked out the door towards him. Johnnie was standing on the grass with his strong sunglasses on. After he had answered the doctor's question about his health favourably, Angus came straight to the point. He was a little nervous but he was determined to get to the root of the mystery.

"Johnnie, I was a bit surprised at the very light colour of your blood yesterday. Has it always been like that?"

Johnnie raised his shoulders and opened his arms and palms to indicate "Don't know."

"I was so surprised, I put some blood-soaked cotton wool in my bag. My hobby is haematology and I looked at it under the microscope."

Immediately, Johnnie's eyes and demeanour changed. He looked very alert and slightly unsettled. "Now why would you want do a thing like that?" he asked with a severe frown. Not a friendly look.

"I wanted to look at it, obviously." He looked Johnnie in the eye and announced baldly, "It's not the blood of a human being," waiting to see the reaction.

Johnnie crossed his arms and his expression was as cold as ice. He thought to himself he could do without this. What with Andreas' earlier visit threatening his continuation on the project and now this damned man in a position to blow the whole thing, it was all too much.

"Have you told anyone else about this?"

"No."

"Are you _absolutely_ sure."

"Yes. I wanted to confront you and get your explanation first."

Johnny took his sunglasses off and stared very hard at Angus. A bit like the stare he gave Jimmy Basher, but different. He was hypnotising him – deeply. Angus stood stiffly still, his eyes were glazed and he was as silent as a lamb.

"You're not going to get an explanation. I'm very sorry to do this to you, Angus, but I've got no choice. There's no hard feelings on my part. You didn't realise the possible effect of what you've done." Dr. Maclennan couldn't move his eyes away from Johnnie's magnetic gaze.

"You will forget everything about the blood, your examination of it and the results. Forever. You will forget this and believe our discussion today was bland and mundane. Just about my cut. Furthermore, you will go straight home immediately and burn the cotton wool. If you have written any notes, you will destroy them too. Is this fully understood?"

Angus nodded robotically.

"When I turn my eyes away in two seconds you will come out of your trance."

Dr. Maclennan walked back into the house, said goodbye to Catriona and quickly headed straight back home.

"Thank God he didn't tell anyone else," thought Johnnie. "What next? Everything seems to be unravelling."

Chapter 7

One fine but cool, clear day in the school holidays, Catriona announced it was time to cut peats to keep them all going with fuel throughout the winter months. She had paid the local council the nominal rental of seven and sixpence for their own patch of peat bog at the Breasclete end of Callanish just outside the village. They set off in the Vauxhall Velox, arriving at the spot about half an hour later. Kathy wasn't with them as she was at home playing with a friend. A vertical wall of peat was bare on one side from last year's cutting and that's where they would start.

"I'll show you what to do, Johnnie. We need a cutter and a thrower. Some cutters do the whole job on their own but it's easier with two people. Calum can cut – he's done it before. Johnnie, you stand in the bog, catch the peats as they're cut and throw them up on the turf. Before that, I'll cut off the top three-inch layer of turf and heather with this spade for us to reach the peat layer and get started."

When she'd done this, she handed Calum the cutting tool, called a tarasgeir (tara-sker). It had a wooden handle with a T at the top, but instead of a spade blade it had a narrow eighteen-inch-long steel blade coming out at right angles to the handle. It wasn't very sharp. That's unnecessary and dangerous. Quite blunt in fact. Merely sharp enough to slice through the soft, sodden, black peat. Above the blade, there was also a horizontal foot rest so the operator could push the blade through the peat.

It was hot and thirsty work. The hardest job is being the thrower. Each slice of peat is about fifteen inches square and four inches thick. The water content is huge, so when they fully dry out, they reduce to about nine inches square and two inches thick and lose nearly all their weight through evaporation. They also change colour from black to mid-brown. However, the newly-cut, black peat is heavy and Johnnie's clothes became more and more filthy and saturated as the day progressed. They stopped after about 3 hours' solid work at around 1 pm, lying on the dry heather, eating their picnic with the sun reviving their bodies and spirits. Another two hours in the afternoon was enough for them. Johnnie was the only one who was very dirty. The other two were comparatively clean. Catriona had brought a clean set of clothes for Johnnie and Calum.

"What's the next step with the peats?" asked Johnnie.

"We'll come back a few more times and cut some more." replied Catriona. "Then we'll return two weeks later and turn them all over to let the sun get at the other side. Then a fortnight after that we put them in little raised stacks of four, leaning the edges against each other, so they get air on every side. Another two weeks after that I'll get one of our neighbours, Tommy Smith, who has a lorry, to come here and we'll throw all the peats on the back. When they get dumped on the street outside our house, all the neighbours come round and help carry them round the back of the house, where I make them into a stack, shaped like a loaf. Then, I throw an old tarpaulin over the top to keep most of the rain off. By the time September comes round, they're dry enough to use. If there are any left from last year, they're even better. They're even drier, harder and denser, so they burn better."

You can both have a bath at Dolligan's and change into your clean clothes. A good wash will do me. I haven't been doing as much work as you two." So they got back in the car and Catriona drove to her uncle's house.

After everyone had cleaned themselves up, they all sat down to high tea at about 5.30 pm, the big meal of the day. Murdo had driven from Stornoway to join them and was already sitting on the settee with an amused, cocky grin on his face.

"Can't beat a bit of healthy exercise to give you an appetite, eh, Johnnie? Sorry I couldn't be there to give you a helping hand," he lied with mock regret. Catriona shook her head but chuckled at the same time.

Mairi had made boiled new potatoes, carrots and peas with fillets of herring, coated in oatmeal and shallow fried in the frying pan. Untraditionally, she had made a gooseberry sauce to go with it. "I saw the recipe in "Women's Own" last week," Mairi explained. "We've got a few wild gooseberry bushes at the back of the house, so I thought I'd give it a try." Johnnie had a salad, but as usual didn't eat much. Afterwards, the others all had home-made sultana scones with butter and strawberry jam and a cup of tea, while Johnnie sipped some black tea. Everyone expressed delight with the meal and sat round the fire. "That gooseberry sauce was great, Mairi. The sharpness cuts through the fattiness of the fried fish," commented Catriona, who loved her food.

Calum wiped his mouth with his paper napkin. "Uncle Dolligan, why don't you tell some more strange Lewis tales. Johnnie really likes them."

"OK. How about the Flannan Isles Mystery?"

When Calum nodded vigorously, Dolligan re-lit his pipe slowly. He leant forward, rested his elbows on his knees and announced melodramatically in a slow, deep voice, "This is a mystery which has taxed the brains of many clever men but has never, ever been solved." Calum settled comfortably into his chair as they all listened attentively. "It happened at Christmas time in the year 1900." Turning to Johnnie, he explained "The Flannan Isles are seven tiny, uninhabited islands 20 miles west of Lewis off the coast of Uig. The largest is called Eilean Mor ("big island") although it's still very small. It's beachless with steep cliffs all round and there's a lighthouse on it.

Before Christmas, it was noticed from Uig that the light had gone out. However, due to fierce, stormy weather, the boat "Hesperus," due to be sent from Uig to relieve the three keepers and find out what had gone wrong, couldn't sail until Boxing Day. Normally a flag would be flown from the lighthouse, to acknowledge the incoming boat. The lighthouse crew would come out onto the jetty to help the three men up from the rowing boat sent from the "Hesperus"."

However, no flag could be seen. Back on the "Hesperus" they blew the ship's whistle………..still no sign of the keepers, James Ducat, Thomas Marshall and Donald MacArthur. Surprised and puzzled, they had to negotiate the landing themselves in the rolling seas. Strangely, the rails on the jetty were badly twisted. They made their way to the lighthouse in puzzled silence. There was an uncanny atmosphere of dread and foreboding. As they listened for any sign of the men, all they could hear was the crashing of the waves on the rocks below and the angry squawking of the gulls above. The birds were going bananas as if they were telling the men something was wrong. There was little wind but the moist air was salty and bitterly cold. They opened the lighthouse door, which was unlocked, then made their way up the stairs to the living room. This door was locked and when they opened it, a strange sight awaited them.

The room was deserted. Not a soul. The clock on the wall had stopped at exactly the same time as every other clock in the building. Strange, eh? Anyway, the fire had obviously gone out and there was an unfinished meal of cold meat, bread and cheese on the table. One chair had over-turned on to the floor. As if they'd been disturbed mid-meal by a sudden emergency. They listened for any sounds, but all they heard was the pitiful, weak cheeping of a canary in a cage, half-starved on its perch. Upstairs, the beds were neatly made, but empty. The men searched everywhere. Not a dicky-bird. The keepers had disappeared into thin air." Dolligan's face was sombre. "The atmosphere all over the lighthouse had an ominous, doleful feel to it, a kind of supernatural dread."

He resumed the story after a long draw on the pipe. "The Head Keeper's log stated there had been a savage storm on 14th December, although it had calmed down by the following day when the final log entry was made. It was short and sweet. "Storm ended, sea calm. God is over all"."

Dolligan paused to relight his pipe again, wafting fruity, sweet-smelling smoke round the room. The peats crackled in the grate. All eyes were on him, waiting for him to resume the tale.

"The legend is that when the men from the "Hesperus" looked all round the island, desperately seeking clues, they saw three huge, black, weird-looking, ugly birds of unknown species silently and uncannily staring back at them from the rocks. They were too big for seabirds." Narrowing his eyes, he turned his head slowly to Johnnie. "They looked more like three lighthouse-men sitting bolt upright."

Dolligan took another long draw on his pipe. "A few days later, Robert Muirhead, the superintendent in charge of the case sailed from Lewis to the island to carry out an official investigation. He said the storm on the night of 14th December had clearly caused the jetty rails to become bent out of shape. Great rocks had been dislodged and thrown around like pebbles, and ropes had become entangled on a temporary crane 70 feet above, so that's maybe what damaged the rails. Two of the keepers' waterproof oilskins and boots were missing with one man's still remaining, neatly hung up. The investigator gave his solution to the mystery. He assumed that all three men had left the lighthouse to re-secure the equipment. A huge wave had rolled in and washed them into the sea. Once they were in the churning water, they were soon drowned and their bodies carried miles out to sea. Officially, that was that.

Dead simple, eh? You're joking. There were loads of unanswered questions. Why had one of them left behind his oilskins and boots in the wet, stormy, freezing December weather? Why did they lock the living room door as they went out? If they were in such a rush that they overturned a chair, why waste time locking up? Who were they trying to keep out? If they died in the sea, why were <u>none</u> of their bodies ever washed up anywhere? Why did they <u>all</u> leave the building? One of the unbreakable regulations in the official rule-book states clearly that one person should always wait behind, irrespective of the level of the emergency. It was a strict taboo that had never been broken before.

What's more, what about the strange entry in the keeper's log on the 12th December. Thomas Marshall recorded "severe winds, the likes of which I have never seen before in twenty years. James Ducat has been very quiet and William Macarthur has been crying." Why? These were seasoned, experienced lighthouse men so it wasn't fear. They must have known there was no danger from high seas or stormy winds inside a solid, sturdy, newly built lighthouse many feet above the ground. Alternatively, had the two fallen out, perhaps? Ducat was a gentle giant, sober and thoughtful. Very reliable and conscientious. Macarthur, on the other hand, was a bit of a drinker onshore who sometimes got involved in a bar brawl. The two didn't always see eye to eye apparently, but I suppose it's a big leap from that to three deaths.

Many said the police report was a whitewash to keep other lighthouse keepers from getting too frightened. Some suggested the work of the devil or a massive sea-monster dragging the three keepers to their deaths. More recently, some say a UFO abducted them from Eilean Mor. Others thought one of the keepers had gone mad and killed the others, pushed them into the sea and then dived in himself. Apparently, there's a history of lighthouse keepers going mad.

Wilfrid Gibson wrote a poem about it all. It's really spooky. I know the final verse off by heart:

We seem'd to stand for an endless while,
Though still no word was said,
Three men alive on Flannan Isle,
Who thought on three men dead."

"Another thing," Dolligan lowered his voice and spoke in hushed tones with a histrionic, knowing look, "for years afterwards, keepers at Eilean Mor reported eerie, wailing voices in the wind." He paused ominously......."They were calling out the names of the dead men."

Everyone sat completely still for a few seconds. Calum coughed nervously. Mairi shivered and pulled her cardigan closer to her body.

Quickly pulling herself together, it was Mairi who moved first. She got up and added a few fresh peats to the fire from the basket beside the hearth, sparking as they touched the hot embers. They had all sat through the story without interruption, enthralled by Dolligan's theatrical story-telling and intimate knowledge of the tale. By now, evening had arrived and the temperature had dropped considerably outside. However, that was kept firmly at bay by the warmth of the roaring fire.

Johnnie clapped his hands in admiration. "Wonderful story! You should do this professionally. You're a natural. I can see how you Lewismen enjoyed your nights round the fire in winter. Any more local tales?"

"How about the "The Iolaire," Dolligan?" suggested Calum with relish.

"OK," responded the old man. Clearing his throat, Dolligan set the scene.

"Six thousand men, twenty per cent of the total population of Lewis at the time fought in the First World War," he began slowly. "One in five of those never returned. Per head of population, it was the highest death rate of any small area of Great Britain. On New Years Day 1919, nearly three hundred sailors in the Royal Naval Reserve were returning to Stornoway in high spirits on the "Iolaire,", a large, privately-owned luxury yacht commandeered by the Royal Navy during the war. The relatives and womenfolk were waiting to welcome their men home, relieved they'd survived the war."

Murdo interrupted informatively to say that "Iolaire" means "eagle" in Gaelic.

"Mairi, pass me that red book with the gold lettering" indicated Dolligan. "Thanks, Mairi. This describes it better than I would. I can't remember all the finer details." Dolligan read from the book:

"The New Year celebrations were in full swing as the "Iolaire" sailed through the Minch. They saw the light at Arnish Point, and the sparkling lights of Stornoway harbour and they looked forward to landing. The "Iolaire" passed a small fishing boat on its approach to the harbour entrance. The channel is only about 750 yards wide, so the pilot needed to be very careful as the yacht had never made this trip at night before. What happened in the next few minutes will never be fully understood as Commander Mason and the navigator, Lieutenant Cotter did not survive. Nor did all but five of the rest of the crew. It was plain that the weather had worsened, with sleet showers whipping across on a strong southerly - but not enough to affect navigation. However, soon after 1am, disaster came with a vengeance. The "Iolaire" suddenly struck the rocks known as The Beasts of Holm.

It was a moonless night and in the pitch darkness, no-one on board had any precise idea where they were until the first distress rockets were fired. The Iolaire was lying only twenty yards from land, but with a boiling sea raging between the stricken vessel and the rocky shore and the hellish darkness no-one knew this. Many men immediately filled the two lifeboats, and drowned as they were swamped by the huge waves. A heavier rope was attached and a loop was made around a rock to hold it fast and the men took it in turns to stabilise the rope until, exhausted, others would take their place.

Just before the "Iolaire" finally sank, three men made a desperate attempt to climb the masts. Two climbed the for'ard mast and young 20-year old Donald "The Patch" Morrison climbed the mizzen mast. The storm continued to smash into the disintegrating wreck and at about 5 am the foremast snapped and Donald was left alone clinging on for dear life. Incredibly, The Patch survived the night at the top of the mast and was rescued the next morning at 10am having spent at least 8 hours in freezing temperatures and in the most awful conditions. He spent only a day in hospital but his brother Angus did not survive. Controversy surrounded the rescue attempts, as the Court of Inquiry that took place in Stornoway in February revealed. Although the evidence presented made it clear that no help had been possible from the sea, it emerged that the lifeboat crew could not be roused. The island was rife with rumour as the inquiry proceeded - why had the ship sunk so close to home? Who was responsible? The fact that it occurred on New Year's Eve led to the understandable assertion that the officers had been under the influence of drink. This was not borne out by any of the witnesses however, and it seems clear that none of the officers involved gave any indication of intoxication.

The conclusion of the Public Enquiry was "that the officers in charge did not exercise sufficient prudence in approaching the harbour; that the boat did not slow down, and that no look out was on duty; and that the number of lifebelts, boats and rafts was insufficient for the number of people carried," The criticism of the Navy's response was implicit in their recommendations that drastic improvements be made in the conveyancing of life-saving apparatus and "that the Government should in future provide adequate and safe travelling facilities for Naval ratings and soldiers". Not much consolation to the 58 widows and over 200 children left fatherless by the disaster."

Dolligan read on. "The Navy was quite rightly held responsible for the inept response to the accident. However it is doubtful how much could have been done given the nature of the wreck and its location. Almost unbelievably however, the Admiralty offered the wreck for sale 15 days after the disaster, with 88 bodies still unaccounted for. This crass insensitivity did nothing but increase the feeling of the islanders that their men had been treated with contempt, when so many of them had served so long and with such distinction. 205 men were lost that night; whole communities were devastated. Two families of eight children left fatherless, two of seven children; four pairs of brothers died..

Then there's the story of the woman who had prepared food and a fire for the return of her husband. Her daughter fell asleep shortly after midnight, to awake six hours later. The fire was out, and the food lay cold on the stove. The mother was in a great state of distress, and she said "I am a widow," although no one had as yet arrived to break the news. Church elders were seen in the village at daybreak, to confirm the awful news."

An unbearable, desperately cruel tragedy occurred that dark Hogmanay night off the Isle of Lewis. These words from the 10th January 1919 edition of the Stornoway Gazette sum it up.

"No-one who is now alive in Lewis can ever forget the 1st of January 1919, and future generations will speak of it as the blackest day in the history of the island, for on it over 200 of the bravest and the best perished on the very threshold of their homes under the most tragic circumstances. The terrible disaster at Holm has plunged every home and every heart in Lewis into grief unutterable."

Dolligan closed the book and placed it on the table beside him exhaling a thespian sigh. He then removed his spectacles, replaced them in their case and slowly placed the case on top of the book. Dramatic to the last.

After a few seconds, Murdo broke the silence with a deadpan face. "Well, that's cheered us all up no end, Dolligan. Just as well we don't have a gas oven."

Dolligan knotted his brow and eyed Murdo scornfully, "Well, you can scoff, Murdo, but melancholy's part of the Gaelic character. That's why we love mournful songs and sad tales and all that sort of thing."

"That's because we can't get over losing our country and our soul to the English," said Murdo with feeling. "Gaels have a bit of a split personality. Flair and bravery on one hand, but a self-destruct button on the other. Bonny Prince Charlie was a total loser. Why would anyone with a brain have risked their lives for him?"

"Oh yeah?" Dolligan riposted. "Him and his army got as far as Derby. The government in London thought their time had come."

"Yeah, that's right. And then what did the stupid, wee sod do? Just when he had them on the run, he led the army all the way back to Scotland. What's the bloody point of that? The tactics at Culloden were crap too. The whole shebang was a bit like a football match. We were 3-0 up at half-time, then the captain lost his nerve and blew it in the second half."

"Aye, we lost the long battle with the English in the end," mourned Dolligan. "After Culloden, the clans were broken up. Neutered. And tartan was banned, too."

Johnnie shook his head. "In the short term, you're absolutely right. There were many horrible atrocities and hardships for years afterwards. It was appalling. A huge disaster for the Highlanders. The Duke of Cumberland took his revenge in blood and he wasn't called "The Butcher" for nothing. However, in the long term, without Culloden, there would have continued to be uprisings and disunity and the British Empire would never have flourished. The combination of the Scots united with the English, together with the other home countries, was an unstoppable force. The Scots regiments are admired all over the world. "The ladies from hell" and "devils in skirts," as the Germans used to call them. What's more, a huge number of Scots served in prominent administrative posts abroad. They practically ran the empire."

"Hmph," said Murdo "Was the British Empire really as good a thing as everyone seems to think?"

"It's fashionable today to run it down."

"With bloody good cause, too." Murdo spat the words out angrily. "The reason the sun never set on the British Empire was that God didn't trust the British in the dark."

Johnnie gave a disparaging smile. "Very amusing, Murdo. I can't deny the short-term results of the defeat were appalling. Highlanders were treated as an inferior species. Later, the British troops collectively treated the defeated native peoples with the same disdain. At any point in history, the people at the top of the pile always believe those below them are inferior by nature, not just by accident of circumstance. Time and the inexorable cycle of fortune soon dispel their illusions."

The others smiled at the overweening, elaborate, old-fashioned turn of phrase. Johnnie loved waxing lyrical. They were all used to it by now.

Johnnie continued. "According to Peter Hitchens, a shrewd journalist, author and political commentator in the next century, "In this world, you either have an empire or you're part of somebody else's. And if you had to choose to be in any of the empires of the past two thousand years, I think the British Empire would come high on the list." Few could argue with that. The Pax Britannica left behind new systems of law and democratic institutions. It's dead easy to criticise centuries or even decades after events. You have to judge people in the context of when they lived."

"You mean like criticising Genghis Khan for not being a supporter of Amnesty International?" cracked Calum.

Johnnie laughed. "I like it. No, a more serious example would be Thomas Jefferson. Few today would criticise him too strongly for using slave labour in the 18th century, although they would be rightly outraged if he did it today."

"Mind, if he <u>had</u> refused to use slaves in his own century, he would have been an even better man," riposted Murdo sarcastically.

"That's very true. But, then again, nearly everyone is a creature of their time. Few people in any generation are so noble and ahead of their time that they transcend their own era. There will be a black man from South Africa at the end of this century who will forgive his captors and oppressors not only after the event, but also during his long persecution. Even his jailers will be literally transformed by his wise judgement and unwavering humanity. A true leader. Arguably, the greatest man of the twentieth century. He will be released as an old man, and then become President of his country and his calm, thoughtful fairness, his far-sighted vision and determination will probably prevent thousands of deaths. Without him, some of the black Africans, roused to revenge by their cruel, unfair treatment in the past would probably take revenge on the whites violently. What's more, one of the main reasons the whites will agree to give up some of their power is their faith in this man, that he would make sure the transition was controlled and peaceful for all. Their faith will be well-founded. A great man, ahead of his time. Unfortunately, his successors will squander his legacy. It's a pity he won't be alive a few decades later when the times are monumentally tougher all over the world."

"Ach…more prophecies!" exclaimed Murdo, shaking his head, and adding disbelievingly "We'll see when the time comes."

Johnnie then changed the subject, "Do you fancy a walk round to the Stones, Calum?" Surprised after Johnnie's previous reluctance to take him along, Calum eagerly accepted.

"You'd both better wrap up warm. I'll get you a scarf each to tuck into your jackets. Put these caps on as well," offered Mairi. "Although it's summer, it can still get pretty cold at night."

Johnnie and Calum left the house into a bright, still but cool evening light with long shadows. Summer days at this latitude are long. On a clear night in the middle to end of June, you can read a newspaper inside the house at midnight in Lewis without the light on. As they made their way to the megaliths, Calum waited for Johnnie to speak first. He was intrigued why they were going. Johnnie rarely did anything without a reason.

After fully half a minute, Johnnie broke the silence. "Remember you asked me what happened last time I went to the stones? Well, you're about to find out." Calum said nothing. When they reached the stones, Johnnie took off the medallion-like object hanging from his neck and held it in his left hand. Calum had noticed the medallion before but thought it was merely decorative. Johnnie told him to copy what he did. Johnnie put his right palm against the stone where the vertical Grand Avenue intersected the horizontal arm of the cross. Calum followed with his left as Johnnie held Calum's right hand in his left, placing both their palms round the medallion against the stone. The medallion began to emit a narrow pencil of blue light directly upwards into the heavens. A wind started and picked up speed, spinning faster and faster. Lightning cracked the sky. Calum was afraid but didn't want to back off. He was fascinated, scared and elated at the same time. His head was spinning. The air churned wildly and a blinding, whirling light spun round them like a whirlwind. Then..... Calum blacked out and both of them disappeared completely in an instant.

He woke up later sitting with his back to the stone. He felt disorientated as if coming out of a dream. Johnnie was sitting in the same position against the opposite stone, watching him with a slight grin on his face.

"So you're back then?"

"Yes, but I'm a bit groggy"

"You'll be alright, don't worry."

"What happened? Where have we been?

"Somewhere else."

"Whereabouts is "somewhere else?"

"Work it out."

Calum looked at his watch. He was shocked. It was well over an hour since they arrived at the stones. They made their way back to Dolligan's and after a cup of tea, everyone set off back to Stornoway. Again, both Calum and Johnnie were very subdued.

The following morning, after breakfast, they both went for a walk along Culagrein.

"I had a very strange dream last night. Only…..it was like the real thing. Very realistic," said Calum.

"Thought you might. What happened in it?"

"I felt as if I was flying. Very fast. Over fields and hills and lakes, but I didn't recognise where it was. It wasn't like anywhere I'd ever seen. I passed over open countryside and towns too with tall glass buildings. Strange trees and plants with weird, unusual colours. Like something out of a science fiction book. There was something very different about the place. At first, I couldn't work it out. Then I realised what it was. Although the sun was fully out and there were no clouds, the light was very subdued. A bit like twilight. How could that be? After a while, the scene changed. I arrived at a huge glass building. I was in a room with about half a dozen strangers who looked like you. Tall and thin - some even taller and thinner than you. In fact, I could swear you were there with them."

Johnnie grinned. "Of course I was there. And I was given some good news about a decision by the elders on my planet. They'd criticised me for killing Jimmy Basher and they'd called a meeting to discuss my future on my project here on Earth. Thankfully, I was vindicated and told to carry on as usual."

"Really? Thank goodness for that. You must have been worried." Then he realised something. "Hang on, with your prophetic skills, couldn't you have foreseen the result?"

Johnnie laughed. "It doesn't work like that, thank goodness. I can only see certain things. One of the things I can't foresee is my own future. If I could, normal life would be impossible."

"How did they know exactly what had happened with Jimmy Basher?"

"I wear two tiny cameras embedded in my clothing all the time…..and I mean tiny. About the size of a pin-head. One at the front and one at the back. They record everything and transmit to them live as it happens. They also pick up sound. I'm not just abandoned here on my own, you know. It's an important and controversial project and there's a back-up team at home, watching developments all the time."

"Crikey, that's really clever!" Calum went on with his story. "Anyway, they were asking some questions but mainly they were doing the talking, showing me things in 3-D holographic movies with stereophonic sound. It's like looking at a play in a theatre but the figures obviously look much smaller, about a foot high. Absolutely mind-blowing! Because they saw I was so incredibly fascinated by the technology and that I love history, they did something special for me. They showed me a 3-D holographic movie actually filmed by some of their people at the Battle of Waterloo. Actual events, not actors. The real thing, recorded as it happened. I've never seen anything so exciting in my life. With close-ups of Wellington and Napoleon, who looked ill and ashen-faced. You know he was in great pain with severe duodenal ulcers, don't you? It may have cost him the battle. He had to rest for short periods during the fighting."

"I know. You were totally blown away by it!" he said, laughing. "What other stuff do you remember?"

"You were there, so you should know. I can't remember everything exactly. They said they'd make me forget most of what I'd been shown for now but the knowledge would be implanted in my brain and it would help me in the future. They obviously didn't block the Waterloo recording from my mind. Presumably because it was just a bit of fun for my benefit, not part of the serious, important lecture. The impression I have is that the serious stuff was to do with fascinating events to come. Many were really disturbing. It's to do with our visit to the standing stones yesterday, isn't it?" With his eyes fixed on Johnnie, he added, "I obviously went to where you come from, didn't I?"

"That's right, Calum."

"Somewhere else. Somewhere very different."

"Yes."

"Or maybe <u>somewhen</u> else?"

"That too."

"The word "symbiosis" kept coming up during my dream. What does it mean?"

"It has a technical scientific meaning." After a moment's thought, he added "but metaphorically it just means……..well…. remember I was talking the other day about why I was here. I said to teach and learn at the same time?" Calum nodded

"Well, that's a kind of symbiosis. Mutual help."

"Explain more to me about exactly where you come from?"

"No, sorry. You have no need to know." His face crinkled a grin and he put a reassuring hand on Calum's shoulder. "Don't worry, I promise just before I go back home, I'll explain fully why I'm here and much more besides. Really important things that'll surprise and fascinate you. Some will shock you."

Chapter 8

Summer turned inevitably into autumn. The leaves developed gold and russet tones and the air cooled. One Friday morning in late September, a head popped round the kitchen door.

"Hello there, Catriona," said a tall, broad-shouldered, short-haired, red-headed man in police uniform. He was in his early forties, heavily built, with a tough, pock-marked face, the legacy of a bad acne problem in his youth.

"Hello, Sergeant Drummond. How are you?" acknowledged Catriona.

Drummond bridled at her use of his surname. "Why d'you always call me that? Why don't you call me Jock, like everyone else? We've known each other long enough."

"It's out of respect for your rank," she lied. The truth was she disliked him intensely, as did the rest of the family. However, she didn't want him to know that. He was a man to have on your side - or at the very least, not as your enemy. A crafty troublemaker. Although by far the greatest emotion she felt was dislike, underneath, she also felt sorry for him in a funny sort of way. He had few friends because he was one of those people who repel others. People sensed something malign and cunning about him and knew he didn't care for anybody except himself. Constable Maclean, a very popular bobbie in the community, who worked under Drummond, described him as "a bit like Attila the Hun….but without the charm."

From a dysfunctional, poor family with a violent and drunken father, Drummond had been determined to rise above this and worked hard at school. Although not academic, he was very shrewd and intelligent in a non-academic way. He applied and was accepted as a policeman when he left school at sixteen. His shrewdness and assiduous hard work resulted in his rising to sergeant quite quickly, strictly on merit. Then he hit a brick wall. Although grudgingly respected by his superiors, his inability, despite his prodigious natural intelligence, to pass exams and his unprepossessing, sour manner and lack of people-skills caused him to be turned down in applications for inspector rank. Three times. Officers of inferior ability were promoted ahead of him. As a result, he became resentful, making his bitter disposition worse. Like a vicious circle.

He popped round to see Catriona every so often, usually because he was after some information and also because, unlike many people, she was pleasant and civilised with him.

"I bet you've got some Banjos in that biscuit barrel. They'd be nice with a cup of tea."

"You're so subtle. Milk and two sugars?"

Grinning broadly, Drummond came in and sat at the table. When the tea was ready, she passed over the biscuit barrel. He was fond of chocolate biscuits. Catriona knew he was after something but she was determined not to give him the satisfaction of asking why he had come. Soon enough, he raised the issue.

"Is Johnnie Quiet still staying here?" Then a pause. "Looks a bit of a weirdo to me."

"What would you know about him, sergeant? He's a very decent man and helps us out a lot."

"I'm very suspicious about his background. I want to speak to him. Is he in?"

Catriona's heart sank. She hoped he was not going make things difficult for Johnnie. "He's round the back. I'll get him for you." She dried her hands with a tea-towel and started to move towards the back door, but Johnnie was already there, impassive in his facial expression as ever.

"Don't worry, Catriona," he intoned flatly, cleaning his hands of paint with a rag. "I overheard some of the conversation. What can I do for you, Sergeant Drummond?"

He sat at the other end of the table as Catriona left the room out of courtesy.

"What's your proper name?"

"Jan Larsen. Johnnie's an Anglicised version."

"Where are you from?"

"Oslo."

"Hmm. Can I see your passport?"

Johnnie got up and went into his bedroom and after re-emerging, he handed it over with a with a dead-pan expression.

Drummond looked at him with distaste and suspicion. He flicked through the passport. "I'm going to go through it at the station with a fine tooth-comb."

Drummond's manner was very threatening and leaning forward in his chair, he said disdainfully, "I don't believe you're who you say you are. I've heard some spooky rumours about you. So..........I'm going to look into your background very carefully." Tapping the side of his nose with an exaggerated knowing look, he grinned maliciously. "Got a friend in MI5. Went on a course with him once and we've kept in touch." The grin went quickly and his eyes now burrowed into Johnnie's. "You do know you're not allowed to stay in this country indefinitely, don't you?" Johnnie looked him unwaveringly in the eye but remained as poker-faced as the sphinx.

Rising purposefully from the table, Drummond turned as he reached the back door, staring menacingly at Johnnie and pointed his index finger at him. "See you again very soon, Mr Larsen."

When Calum came back from school just after 4 o'clock, both his mother and Johnnie told him the story.

Taking the boy to one side, he put his hand on his shoulder. "We need to talk tonight urgently, Calum. Your mother's going round to see Alina this evening, so we can have a private chat then."

After the evening meal, Catriona set off for Alina's and Johnnie and Calum sat down facing each other at the kitchen table. "Calum, I've always told you I'm not here forever. Only for a short period. I've accomplished what I came here for, bar one thing, the most important part. To explain everything to you. Then my mission here is completed." Calum's spirits sank and Johnnie picked up the vibes. He felt sorry for him. Give him something to occupy him, he decided.

"Why don't you make us both a cup of tea, Calum?"

Calum rose from the chair and filled up the kettle as Johnnie sat back, raised his arms and put his hands behind his head. Completely relaxed, compared to the boy who was down in the dumps.

"The time has come for me to go. If I've judged Drummond right, he's going to dig very deep. In any case, as I said, my job's done here, so I would have been going soon anyway. Tomorrow's as good a time as any."

"But, Johnnie........," protested Calum loudly with a tear in his eye. He knew in his heart though that Johnnie's mind was made up.

"Listen very carefully to everything I have to say. It's very important. We only have a few hours and I need to explain the whole thing to you. There's quite a lot to tell you, in fact. The reason I came to the island was to teach you and learn from you and others. I needed to learn and understand more about the human race so that I can help them better. Even more importantly, I also need to prepare you for a traumatic time to come when you're much older. During your recent trip to where I come from, you were taught an enormous amount about this, even although your conscious mind can't remember much. You'll need all this in the future, when things have deteriorated to a degree you couldn't comprehend today."

"Deteriorated? In what way?"

"Winston Churchill coined a wonderful metaphor. So good, that I've memorised it - as usual. He was talking about Britain before the Second World War, but it could apply equally well today to Western civilisation as a whole." Pausing to concentrate, Johnnie quoted:

"I have watched this famous island descending incontinently, fecklessly, the stairway which leads to a dark gulf. It is a fine broad stairway at the beginning, but after a bit the carpet ends. A little farther on there are only flagstones, and a little farther on still, these break beneath your feet."

Johnnie continued "W.B. Yeats foresaw a terrible time when "Things fall apart; the centre cannot hold, Mere anarchy is loosed on the world, ... the best lack all conviction, while the worst are full of passionate intensity." The poem's called "The Second Coming," and you must read it. It's quite short but it's really good. A bit scary too."

"How far along Churchill's stairway are we, then?"

"Still on the carpet, but approaching the flagstones. The further you go, the more the speed picks up. The barbarians aren't at the gates yet, but you can hear the noise of them forging their swords from afar. In your lifetime, they'll set off on the long journey that leads to the walls of your cities."

Calum put the tea and hot water in the pot, He was all ears as Johnnie sat forward in his chair and leant his elbows on the table.

"There are many different, mysterious, natural cycles in the world. Many things in life that seem linear are actually cyclical. Part of the secret, arcane Universe. Hidden wheels, if you like.......and even wheels within wheels. And yet some folk say life's just a random accident. Hmph!

Anyway......there's the sixty-year economic cycle on which a Russian scientist called Nikolai Kondratiev proposed a theory in the 1920's and he was quite correct. What's not well-known yet, though, there's also a 500-year geopolitical power cycle. This is obviously a generalisation. It doesn't operate to the exact year or even the exact decade but it does exist nevertheless.

Europe has been the dominant continent for at least a couple of millennia, The beginning of the period from 500BC saw the predominance of city states, particularly in Greece. Meanwhile the power of the Roman Republic was growing phenomenally and completely conquered the whole of the Mediterranean by about 100BC, the height of its power. But after that, it couldn't withstand an uninterrupted series of civil wars between competing military leaders, first Marius and Sulla, then Pompey and Caesar and finally Octavian and Mark Anthony. Octavian emerged the final victor and became the first Roman Emperor just a few years before the birth of Jesus Christ, calling himself Augustus. The Republic was dead. Killed by its own leaders. A bizarre sort of suicide by its own aristocracy.

From the time of Christ until about 500 AD, the Roman Empire took over the mantle of power, reaching its height during the reigns of Trajan, Hadrian and Antoninus Pius. Then came the inevitable decay, and despite a revival under Diocletian and Constantine, things fell apart after the catastrophic defeat against the Goths and Alans at Hadrianople in 378 AD, where the emperor Valens was killed. Rome was sacked twice - in 410 by the Visigoths under Alaric and in 455 by the Vandals under Genseric and the Roman Empire was dissolved literally a few years before 500 AD."

Calum sat silent, fascinated by this novel interpretation of history.

"The Great Wheel ground on and the centre of gravity shifted north. The so called Dark Ages were a period of Germanic and Frankish and finally Viking dominance. The Visigoths colonised France and Spain, the Ostrogoths dominated Italy and the Vandals took over the fertile old Roman colonies in North Africa, but they all eventually had their day. Charlemagne led the Franks and then the Lombards to European dominance. The Vikings completed this northern era, running out of steam around 1000 AD."

"What about Attila the Hun? You haven't mentioned him."

His armies never entered Rome. His main effect on history was that he was a huge catalyst. He swept into Europe from the East, squeezing the Goths and Vandals and forcing them to retreat south. None of the other barbarian peoples could stand up to the Huns, "the scourge of God," as they were known. They were brutal, fierce and unstoppable. All this started to "shake up the jar," and the Goths sought refuge in Rome, where they were not always welcomed or treated well, although they were already converts to Arian Christianity. Their resentment was one of the reasons they rebelled against Rome. Meanwhile, Attila suffered his first ever defeat against a combined Gothic and Roman army at the Battle of Chalons in Gaul. Attila and the remains of his army escaped but were never the same force again. After Attila died soon after, the Huns evaporated completely as a fighting force. Like Alexander the Great, he was a force of Nature and his empire faded away after his death."

Johnnie leant forward and spread hid hands on the table.

"A totally new and very different era dawned in the new millennium, driven by the feudal system and a new kind of warfare. The military pre-eminence of heavily-armoured knights and impregnable castles were the order of the day. In the beginning, the all-conquering and brutal Normans were dominant. However, after about 400 years of continual warfare between armoured knights and archers, the Great Plague suddenly killed off more than a third of the English and European population, which completely unhinged the feudal system. It left a dire shortage of labour, giving workers much greater power and mobility." Johnnie interrupted his narrative and raised an index finger.

"You see, what most people don't realise is that germs have had as much effect on history as conquering armies. For example, a vicious plague was one of the causes of the demise of Carthage at the hands of the Romans, the ancient Athenians at the hands of the Spartans and the sudden collapse of the Hittite Empire some time before that. There have been many other similar examples throughout history. On a mini-scale, you could probably count the helicobacter pylori bacterium which caused Napoleon's duodenal ulcers you mentioned earlier!"

He returned to the narrative.

"At the same time as the feudal system was breaking down, the advent of gunpowder and cannons blew away the ponderous armoured knights and made the castles hard to defend. So, around 1500, the present era came into being with cannons, then guns, and other mechanical weapons, leading later to industrialisation and huge technological advancement. The high civilisations of the West - the Spanish, French and British empires and now America - flowered in great splendour."

Calum carried the pot and two mugs to the table and sat down.

"However. the era of the West is waning fast. All the signs of decay are plain to see. The Great Wheel grinds on slowly but relentlessly. This time, the balance of power is shifting eastwards outside Europe altogether.

William Playfair, a Scottish scientist in the 19th century summed it up perfectly. "Wealth and power have never been long permanent in any place. They travel over the face of the earth, something like a caravan of merchants. On their arrival everything is found green and fresh. While they remain, all is bustle and abundance, and, when gone, all is left trampled down, barren and bare."

All empires go through the same sequence and, as I said, it's plainly obvious Western hegemony is in its final death throes."

He eyed Calum closely. "The people to watch are the Chinese. Very hard working and astute. Arrogant and aggressive too. They have a huge chip on their shoulder about the West, who treated them so brutally and arrogantly in the 19th century. They will never forget their abject humiliation at the hands of the cruel Europeans, "the round-eyed devils," as they called them. You can't blame them. However, they're prepared to wait until the time is ripe. Their shrewd leaders play a very long game. One of them, Zhou En Lai will be asked in 1972 what he thinks the effect of the French Revolution has been on the world. Thinking for a few seconds, he'll reply, "It's too early to tell."

When they grow out of communism, watch out. The Far Eastern bloc led by China will lead the new era and inherit the global Crown of the Ages......or, to be more precise, they'll take it. At the continuous Gargantuan feast of Worldly Power, none of the places have name cards on them. You don't get a polite, printed invitation. If you want to be top dog, you have to grab a seat at the head of the table from the incumbent and dislodge him. He won't just give it to you, you'll have to fight him for it and defeat him. So, the transition period at the end of each era is always full of violence, war and upheaval as the waning and waxing empires collide and then the power and influence shift to the new victor. However, then things slowly settle down to some degree when the new pecking order is established and countries pragmatically accept their new position. However, the new conqueror is no longer an impertinent, jumped-up barbarian. He's the new boss. Get used to it. Meanwhile, the Great Wheel keeps on turning ever so slowly. "

Johnnie took a sip of black tea. He'd grown to like it in his time on the island. Calum was too engrossed to bother with his. "However, there's something crucially different about this present transition. The earth-shattering power of modern weapons of mass destruction - nuclear, biological and chemical. H.G. Wells said that civilisation is in a race between education and catastrophe. Johnnie shook his head. "Sadly, you will lose the race."

In the next century, many weapons of mass destruction will be used. The Four Horsemen of the Apocalypse will have their day. Not surprisingly, the world will take much longer to recover than after previous wars. Massive numbers of people will be killed. More than two billion. Much more than in all previous wars put together. As a result of nuclear and biological contamination, some parts of the earth will be uninhabitable for a long time. Human society will change massively. Although many of the results will actually be very positive and transforming in the long term, before then, it will be cataclysmic for many decades. A huge human tragedy."

"What's all this got to do with me, specifically?"

"You've been chosen for a very important mission."

"What's that, then?"

"There will need to be key people, teachers and doctors, who will help a beleaguered human race to revive, to prevent a decline into total anarchy – and we've identified you as one of these. Don't ask me how we chose you. All you need to know is that we did. Your geographical position will help. Areas remote from big cities, particularly islands, will have a greater survival rate. Learn the lessons I've taught you. Study hard and become knowledgeable as well as wise. We want you to become a doctor and a teacher."

Chapter 9

The conversation had suddenly taken a dramatic turn. Calum was stunned. "So <u>that</u>'s what this whole thing's all about!"

He was silent for about twenty seconds as Johnnie gave him time to let it sink in and recover his equilibrium.

Calum continued, "You mention the Chinese as the biggest threat to the West. They're minnows at the moment. What about the Russians? Don't you think they want a war with the West?"

"They must do. Look how close they put their country to all these American missile bases."

Calum showed a thin sarcastic smile. "So you've been learning a wicked sense of humour since you came here, then."

"That's not really humour, it's irony. The British are the best in world at it. So, I've learned from the masters. Anyway, we digress. The Russians will cause problems all right and there will be many dangerous clashes and local proxy wars, although some will be more widespread, but they won't start a world war. The West are more likely to start one with them! No, in the end, their nemesis will be China. They'll be no match for the Chinese at their peak. The Russians are very brave and good at defending their homeland in a war of attrition with the help of "General Winter." However, when they go to war outside Russia, especially as aggressors, their record is not so impressive. They often lose. Incompetence is part of their national character. Look what the Japanese did to them fifty-odd years ago. They will make trouble for the West, and to be fair, the West will make trouble for them too, but they couldn't defeat the West if they tried. Besides, no country under Communist rule will ever thrive for long."

"But, some of my own views are socialist. Equality for all. How can that be wrong?"

"That's because you're 17 years old. To paraphrase Churchill, "If you're not a socialist at 17, you've got no heart; if you're still one at 35, you've got no brain." Calum looked slightly insulted as Johnnie continued.

"Equality of what, by the way? Equality in the eyes of God? Absolutely. Equality under the law? That's essential. Equality of opportunity? Of course, the nearer you get to this the fairer and more successful a society is. Equality of outcome? No. This can only be achieved by coercion, because it's unnatural and misguided. You need to be given the tools of equality of opportunity. The outcome is then down to you. Your prudence, skill and drive."

"But some people have unfair things holding them back in life."

"We're all born with advantages and handicaps in hundreds of different ways beyond our control. We just have to get on with it. Some people are better-looking than others. So they're usually more popular and more successful in many spheres as a result. How should we equalise that? Give the ugly ones free plastic surgery? Some are more athletic and have greater success in sport. Some are physically more formidable and don't get pushed around or picked on. Some are more intelligent, which is a great predictor of occupational success. When we're born, we're all handed a big bag full of silver spoons and poisoned chalices. Try not to drop it. The secret is to use our advantages to thrive and to overcome our handicaps to stop them holding us back."

He shook his head. "No, Calum, I know what you're thinking. This is not a cruel, unsympathetic philosophy. You can, and should, try to maximise the effects of Nature but you can't defeat it. Nor should you. That's the ultimate in hubris. You should try to help severely disadvantaged people as much as possible, financially and in other ways but not by interfering too much in search of a manufactured, uniform utopia.

"Why is it "greed" to want to keep the money you have earned but not "greed" to want to take somebody else's money?" So said Thomas Sowell, an American political commentator and economist. This is true and one of the troubles with communism is that you eventually run out of other people's money.

Communist countries stifle their own people's abilities, imprison those who disagree with them and put their economies in a straitjacket. In the end, people can't wait to break free. Listen to wise Thomas Sowell again. "Socialism in general has a record of failure so blatantly bad that only an intellectual could ignore or evade it."

Later, Russia will move on from communism but even then they'll be no match for the other Great Powers. They have the worst geopolitical location of any major country in the world. Sandwiched between Western Europe on one flank and the Great Dragon on the other. The almond in a lethal nut-cracker. They're on a hiding to nothing.

As I said, watch the Chinese when they too evolve out of communism. They will be like a whirlwind and led by a young, ruthless, charismatic leader. Contrary to common belief, Russia and China are natural geopolitical enemies and when they square up against each other in the next century, that's the sign the crunch is coming. The Russians will not be able to cope militarily against the Eastern bloc led by the Chinese, who will also be allied to much of Africa and the Moslem countries. Then the West will be dragged in on the side of the Russians. They can't allow such a huge geopolitical shift in the balance of power."

"Won't I be too old when the time comes?"

"No, you will live to a very great age indeed. As well as your intelligence and intellectual capacity being artificially enhanced when you visited my planet, your lifespan was greatly extended too. In fact, your age will be an advantage, not a hindrance."

"Will I ever see you again?"

"Yes. I'll come back to help you when the crunch comes."

"But you're older than me. You'll be dead by then."

Johnnie grinned. "No, I won't. Our life-spans are a lot longer than yours."

"If you can foresee the future so accurately, it must be fixed. Inevitable. How can that be?"

"What I've told you will happen, but it wasn't inevitable. It sounds like a contradiction but it isn't. It's all very complex. As I said before, your understanding of time and dimensions is totally inadequate."

"How did you know I would fall in the river when I did? So you could be there at the right time, I mean?"

"You don't need to know."

"There are loads of different questions I'd like you to answer before you go. On a wide range of subjects."

"Fire away. I'll answer you where I think it's appropriate."

Calum leaned forward in his seat and leant on the table.

"How far are your people ahead of ours?"

"About 500 years, but there are other beings in other places who are thousands....some millions of years ahead. Our people were chosen by a more advanced race to undertake this mission, which is going on all over the world, because we have characteristics and qualities ideally suited for the job. I've personally trained ten people like you all over Northern Europe. I speak twelve European languages fluently." He winked. "Including Norwegian." There are about twenty-five more of us working on this mission in other parts of the world."

"If you know this major disaster is coming, why don't you and your people just stop it?"

"Because all civilisations on every world have to have free will and learn by experience, otherwise they can't truly progress. It's one of the primary rules of the Universe. We only step in to pick up the pieces. We only intervene in a major way after the event to mitigate the effects of your species' actions and get things going again. It's called tough love.

When the big crisis is finally over, your species will reach a new, more advanced state in your spiritual development. The memory of the devastation and lethal war-mongering will be so unbearably traumatic that war and arms will literally be banned. Swords into ploughshares, as the Bible says. All the problems of the world won't be sorted out but a great many will be. Then you'll have to learn how to face the next set of challenges.......but at least without the Sword of Damocles of global annihilation hanging over your head."

"Why did the Supreme Spirit, as you call him, make us so fatally flawed, then?"

"Who knows? In the Book of Life, the answers aren't at the back. However, our people and others on a higher plane than us are actually a lot less critical of you as a species than you are of yourselves."

Calum tilted his head and looked surprised.

"Think about it. You don't know where you come from, why you're here and where you go when you die. If anywhere. Most of Mankind don't even know whether they're alone in the Universe or not. Either alternative is equally terrifying. Blindly fumbling in the dark doesn't even begin to describe the human predicament. The universal ethics and level of spirituality you desperately need both to survive as a species and become a part of the civilised family of different universal species is denied to you because of the animalistic, violent side of your nature which you are saddled with in your genes from birth. Even the very best and most highly-principled of you spend your lives trying to reconcile these two irreconcilable drives."

Johnnie raised a finger to emphasise his points.

"The prevailing theological wisdom for centuries has been that, Mankind were born with everything given to them, but have thrown it all away. This is pure nonsense, a self-flagellatory delusion. On the contrary, you were born significantly imperfect. Blind, dangerously flawed, inchoate, unsophisticated and unprepared, dumped into a brutal, labyrinthine world, red in tooth and claw. I'll concede it's been done this way for good spiritual reasons in your own eventual interest. I truly believe that. Your purpose and challenge are to rise above this, to live a reasonably virtuous, humane and fulfilling life in this bewildering, unfathomable, impenetrable jungle. For the sake of your own soul and the well-being of society, you must try to do this. It's why you're here. As a species collectively, you've had significant successes but, for the time being at least, you've made a bit of a hash of it overall, sadly. However, for anyone to pretend that you were given a favourable kick-start, that you were born with a whole set of silver spoons, is specious sophistry and not supported by the evidence."

"How can we ever progress at all, then?" asked Calum despondently.

"By learning the hard way over time, together with genetically controlling your violent and power-mad impulses, which you will have the technology to achieve in the future. The second half of the next century will be an era of genetic manipulation. A few mistakes will be made because sometimes negative and positive characteristics are two sides of the same coin. For example, when you get rid of unwanted aggression, you have to watch you don't remove drive and the will to succeed. So you need to be incredibly precise but you will learn this science over time.

Marvellous innovations will be achieved in the end. You will discover that most of the people at the very top in politics, the warmongers, the corrupt manipulators, are psychopaths. They have no understanding or feeling for other people's suffering. To them, life's an amoral, egotistical chess game and other people are merely pawns, there to exploit and cheat. They truly can't understand why everybody else isn't like them. This sounds like a cynical exaggeration, but it's not. Look at the hundreds of millions that have been slaughtered by them since civilisation began, with their bloody hands and granite hearts, just to promote their own selfish aims. It's not just Hitler, Mao and Stalin. There have been many, many more and will be in the future.

Psychopathy is a genetically transmitted mental illness which is much more prevalent than you currently think. Many, seemingly ordinary people doing everyday jobs are afflicted with it and make other people's lives a misery with their manipulation and ruthlessness. It ruins their own spiritual development too and it needs to be removed from human genes. As I said, you will be able to eradicate it in the future by genetic manipulation. Another development, emblematic of the same period will be healing by sound waves. The potential is enormous and the medical world will be transformed by it."

Johnnie stared at the tea in his cup, frowning in deep thought.

"Until then, although you don't know it, you are in quarantine as a species. You will not be permitted to reach beyond the moon and Mars until you're fit to join the universal community. You'd be loose cannons. You won't be allowed to wander around the galaxy with your big clumsy boots, knocking over the crockery."

Calum was finding it hard to take everything in. His tea sat untouched on the table.

"Why were we created so vulnerable to self-destruction?"

"We don't know. God knows. Literally. Metaphorically, it's above our pay grade. The ultimate objective will be benign and wise, although it may not always seem so on the surface.

The hierarchy of intelligent beings is like an onion. It's made up of layers. Your layer is further from the centre than ours and we know more about the mysteries of life than you do. We're at a higher level of consciousness, intelligence and spirituality. However there are many other layers nearer the centre than ours. We believe that all beings with souls, which include both you and us, are alive to learn and for their souls to progress to the next stage - whatever that is. The reason we don't know beyond this may be because we're not ready to know or possibly unable to understand it. Would a bird understand what a human being is doing when he puts money in a bank or reads a book. The concepts are beyond its intellectual capacity. Perhaps knowing too much too early in our development would actually screw things up. Disrupt the celestial journey we're on. I strongly suspect it would. Anyway, there'll be a benign logic behind the mystery somewhere."

"Surely the world economy will be destroyed?"

"Of course, but it will recover, slowly at the beginning, but accelerating later. At first, the watchword will be retrenchment. But later the whole economic system will change beyond your present comprehension. Corporate capitalism as you know it today will have become totally discredited. It's too rapacious and causes huge inequality. The very rich totally exploit the poor and enslave them by debt. Similarly, communism will have lost its gloss and credibility for the reasons I told you earlier. It doesn't work, hinders initiative and leads to stagnation - and even greater tyranny."

He picked up the cups, stood up and took them to the sink, then stood with his back leaning against the sink.

"They will both be replaced by what will become known as a "private enterprise" or "PE" economy." Apart from some important government utilities, like energy and public transport, which will be state-run, nothing else will be. There will be two kinds of commercial enterprise. All companies over a certain size based on turnover and number of staff will become a bit like collectives but directly privately owned by the employees individually with mandatory profit-sharing. Employees leaving will have to sell their shares back to the company at the current calculated value. New starters will have to buy shares at the same price. Wages will still vary according to the skills necessary for each job but without the massive differentials of today. Below this size will be private companies, where the employees get mandatory profit-share but don't necessarily hold any shares."

"Isn't this unfair to workers in private companies?"

"No. Don't forget the owners of private companies will be competing with collectives to attract staff so in practice they'll need to offer higher wages and sometimes some equity too in order to entice good staff away from the collectives. The reason for allowing private companies to exist will be to encourage and incentivise entrepreneurs. Society needs their drive, initiative and innovation. If or when they reach the maximum size allowed, private companies will become collectives. The owners will have to sell shares to all the existing employees and when that is exhausted to any others the new collective wants to employ. For a good profit too if the company is an attractive proposition to buy shares in. That's the owners big pay-day in return for their entrepreneurial drive and risk-taking. If the company is not particularly attractive financially, their return will be a lot less. The objective of an entrepreneur will be to build up the company to a peak of profitability, then cash in by what he gets from the eventual sale."

"You say communism doesn't work. But these collectives sound very socialistic to me."

"No, no, no." Johnnie reproved him with an emphatic shake of the head. He walked towards the window and stared out with his hands in his pockets. It was a habit of his when he was making a speech.

"You're not seeing the crucial difference, Calum. I'm surprised at you. Communism has many defects, but there's a "killer" flaw which is the author of all the others - which dooms it to the dustbin of history. The state owns everything, not individual people. Bureaucracy rules and everything stagnates. This is fatal. However, with a PE economy, the great bulk of industry and services is owned by individual people. That's the crucial difference. Think about it. They have an incentive to make things work because they gain personally. What's more, they can't be robbed of their birthright by the machinations of a greedy elite. Political lobbying will be banned. It's outright corruption and manipulation on a grand scale. At the moment, big companies and pressure groups buy or promote their own politicians. The stockmarket won't exist because all the shares are owned by people who work in their companies.

The wealth will be fairly shared. The international central banking system will change completely too……..but that's a long story in its own right. There will be no real poverty. No huge gulf between the top of the pile and the bottom. However, people will still have ample scope to improve their earnings and lifestyle by hard work, skill and prudence, making the economy more dynamic. They'll still have to compete strongly and work hard and if they don't, they won't prosper. You get equality of opportunity without equality of outcome, the ideal model. The outcome's down to your own diligence, industriousness and ability. So, it will be a competitive, vibrant society, but without the manic greed and exploitation of the pre-war order."

"A real utopia then?"

Smiling, Johnnie turned his head and narrowed his eyes as a slight rebuke. He'd picked up the latent sarcasm in Calum's voice.

"You're learning irony yourself, I see. No, there's no such thing as utopia. The drive to create utopia throughout history has been disastrous, leading to awful dystopias instead. So......no. Not utopia, but a very agreeable, peaceful society."

"For how long?"

"A long time, but society won't remain static. It will develop in different ways over time. History moves on. But nothing in the Universe is forever." Johnnie looked out the window at the darkening sky, as clouds moved to cover the moon. "Bad times will return for completely new reasons. However, that's way in the future. Different times, different problems. I see it only dimly."

Calum changed the subject. He was very interested in physics and cosmology. "What about Einstein? Was he right?"

"Like Newton before him, he was right in some ways, but not in others. His theory of the space-time continuum is basically correct but many of his conclusions beyond that are wrong. He was a very interesting man. He said that relativity might be correct or quantum theory might be correct......but not both. He was actually wrong on that one. They're not mutually exclusive. Relativity deals with the macrocosm. How massive objects behave. Quantum theory is about the microcosm. How infinitely small things behave. You'll find the rules are different for each.

He also disagreed with Chaos Theory. He famously said "God doesn't play dice." He was right on that one. Chaos Theory doesn't stack up because there's no such thing as chaos in nature. There's always a complex, hidden order within everything. The fact we can't see it is another matter. He was a great philosopher as well as a scientist. A very benign, humble man too, wasn't he?"

This strange man knows everything, thought Calum with a grin.

"Is there anything important you haven't told me about?"

"Good question, Calum. Good question." Johnnie turned towards him. "Yes. I've not told you in detail about very many things you're not ready to hear. I've had to judge where to put the filters. Not easy. I'm still not sure if I've got it right, but I have to try, anyway. For example, remember I told you about a malign cabal of very powerful men who cause evil events, like assassinations? They're very important and they're so clever and devious, their machinations will not be universally known for a long time. Until it's almost too late."

"Why are you keeping this from me?"

"It would divert you from your true priorities. It would anger you so much, you might want to do something about it too soon. They will be responsible for a huge false-flag event near the turn of the millennium in America. Thousands will be killed. You'll find out when it happens."

"What's a false-flag event?"

"It's when a country carries out a cunning attack or other atrocity in such a way that they can deny it was them and blame an enemy for it. Like the Nazis secretly burning down the Reichstag and blaming the Communists for it to blacken their reputation. For decades, if not longer, it's been a very common standard tactic by major security services all over the world, including the CIA and MI6. Operation Northwoods, proposed secretly by the US military two years ago is a frightening example. It involved killing US citizens, attacking US ships and killing people in US cities but blaming it all on Castro. All to justify an invasion of Cuba. The proposal was spearheaded by General Lemnitzer and signed and endorsed by all the Joint Chiefs of Staff. Although this is being denied at the moment, the existence of this proposal will be admitted publicly in the future. Thank goodness Kennedy rejected it."

Johnnie went back to his chair and leant his chin on his hand with with his elbow on the table.

"Frankly, the military leaders in America and the CIA are way out of control and getting worse all the time. At a top-secret Pentagon "Doomsday Briefing" with Kennedy, just recently, the Joint Chiefs of Staff proposed a pre-emptive nuclear strike on the Soviet Union. Kennedy was horrified and asked General Curtis E. LeMay, Chief of Staff of the US Air Force, to estimate the probable number of deaths on either side. In fact, Kennedy walked out before the end in disgust. Dean Rusk, Kennedy's Secretary of State, said that JFK remarked to him in despair on the way out: "And we call ourselves the human race." LeMay and Lemnitzer, who Kennedy believed is quite literally mentally deranged, have been recommending a pre-emptive strike since Kennedy was elected. Lemnitzer was moved to a new post soon afterwards." Johnnie rubbed his chin.

"Maybe, after all, on reflection, it's a mistake to leave you in the dark on this subject. I've changed my mind. It's too important. I should give you more background, so you can interpret world events better as they progress during your lifetime. But, don't let it deflect you from your primary purpose. That's absolutely paramount."

Calum went to the fridge for orange juice and poured some into a glass. Looking across, he asked, "You want some?" Johnnie nodded, so he poured another one and put it on the table next to him.

"For some time, no-one will be able to do anything about what is effectively an invisible, shadow government in which some of the top military leaders play an important part, together with international bankers, the CIA, huge multi-nationals and others. Not enough people know about what's going on. Public ignorance of the truth is this secret, shadow government's biggest asset." Seeing Calum's expression, he raised his hands. "I know, I know. It sounds outrageous, doesn't it? Nevertheless, before you dismiss it, wait until I've given you the evidence. Provable facts and quotes from famous insiders that will rock you to your very core."

Calum looked shocked as Johnnie went on.

As I say, this is no airy-fairy, off-the-wall theory. There is an abundance of hard evidence if you look for it outside the mainstream media. Many famous prominent people, beginning with that clever Prime Minister, Benjamin Disraeli, have spoken publicly about the situation. However, most revelations have received scant comment in the mainstream press because the cabal own most of them. These whistleblowers actually include at least nine US Presidents, Lincoln, Madison, Jackson, Garfield, McKinlay, both Roosevelts, Eisenhower and Kennedy, who will be the last to stand up to the cabal until well into next century. Also, many vice-presidents, senators, congressmen and a New York mayor. Their comments weren't made out of the corner of their mouth in private. They were said – often bravely - in public or in writing. Just to kick off, Theodore Roosevelt, 26th President of USA, said in his autobiography in 1913:

"Behind the ostensible government sits enthroned an invisible government owing no allegiance and acknowledging no responsibility to the people."

Johnny sipped his orange juice. "It's not easy for a country to return to real democracy after a major, modern war where secrecy and temporary suspension of some freedoms are necessary. To some degree, America succeeded in this after World War One, but not after World War Two.

Crucially, the central banking gangsters, for that's what they are, who occupy the very top of the pyramid, increased their corrupt control after the Second World War. Contrary to the belief of the general public, the Federal Reserve in America is a private company owned by private international bankers, not the government. They have successfully resisted auditing since their inception in 1913 when The Fed was given the monopoly right to issue US currency, creating money they haven't earned from thin air with a flick of the pen and lending it to the government, who have to pay it back with interest."

Johnnie took a longer sip of his orange juice. "All this talking is making me very dry. Are you a bit shocked by all this stuff?"

"Let's put it this way. If it was anyone else telling me this, I would tell them to get a grip. It's a complete eye-opener."

"I'm not surprised, really. Superficially, the UK equivalent to the Fed, The Bank of England, is now owned by the Treasury. Before 1948, it was also a private company owned by the bankers but in that year, it was officially nationalised by Attlee's Labour government to deflect criticism, which didn't suit the international bankers' interests at all. So, in 1977, a subsidiary will be set up called The Bank of England Nominees Ltd. This will be a <u>privately</u> owned company but won't be subject to the normal reporting requirements of the Companies Act. The stated aim of this company will be to hold securities on behalf of certain customers confidentially. This begs a multitude of questions.

Why is the identity of these "investors" confidential? The company will not divulge their identity, even if you ask them. They are not allowed to reveal these investors' names by law. Also, why is this subsidiary necessary at all? Why is it a private company? Why all this secrecy? Also, even though the Bank of England is theoretically state owned, well over 95% of the UK's money supply is privately controlled in the form of interest-bearing loans created by the large commercial banks."

Johnnie shook his head with derision. "You don't have to be a genius to work out things are not quite as straight-forward as they appear at first sight."

Nearly all the national Central Banks in the world are private corporations owned or controlled by this same coterie of corrupt financiers. When some countries refuse to join the interlocked cartel or try to pull out of it, the leaders of these countries are soon discredited or toppled or their country's economy is ruined. Either that, or the country finds itself inexplicably embroiled in a new war.

Savvy politicians have learned it's good life insurance to keep their own counsel. What's doubly shocking in USA is that the Internal Revenue Service, the US tax collecting agency, is also a private corporation unconnected with the government. Controlled by guess who? All US income tax is paid to the Federal Reserve. It's collected by the IRS and sent direct to the Fed, not the Treasury. The IRS is merely the Fed's private collection agency. The Fed's enforcers."

"Could these not just be separate conspiracies, rather than a joined-up cabal?"

"No, I'll develop the case as I go along and show you where everything knits together. Firstly, listen to what Senator William Jenner, said in a speech in 1954:

"Today the path to total dictatorship in the U.S. can be laid by strictly legal means. We have a well-organized political action group in this country, determined to destroy our Constitution and establish a one-party state. It operates secretly, silently, continuously to transform our Government. This ruthless power-seeking elite is a disease of our century. This group is answerable neither to the President, the Congress, nor the courts. It is practically irremovable."

Barry Goldwater, U.S. Senator for Arizona, is no left-wing firebrand. He is an ultra-conservative right-wing Republican. Yet, in his book, "With No Apologies," which will be published in 1979, he will comment on the Trilateral Commission, one of the cabal's think-tanks:

"The Trilateral Commission is international and is intended to be the vehicle for multinational consolidation of the commercial and banking interests by seizing control of the political government of the United States. The Trilateral Commission represents a skilful, co-ordinated effort to seize control and consolidate the four centers of power - Political, Monetary, Intellectual, and Ecclesiastical."

"This all sounds unbelievable! Surely this can't be true? I can't believe the government would allow all this. How come?"

"The government is not in control. The final nail in the coffin of that illusion came in 1913. It was achieved by a mixture of corruption, chicanery and fear. The Federal Reserve Act was passed the day before Christmas Eve in 1913, a day picked deliberately, when most senators were at home with their families. The few who turned up were paid to push it through. Once the deed was done, the bankers weren't going to let it be revoked. They roped in even more senators by corruption. There will be many books written in the future which will describe what's happening but there's one you particularly need to read when it's published. It will explain exactly how the international bankers achieved their goal by artifice, the baleful effect it has had on the world and their ultimate plans. It will be called "The Creature from Jekyll Island," written by a respected journalist called G. Edward Griffin."

Murdo drank from his glass and wrote down the details of the book on a note pad beside him. Johnnie was in full flow.

"Louis T. McFadden, U.S. Congressman and long-time Chairman of the Committee on Banking and Currency for 12 years, pursued the international bankers bravely and resolutely in the 1930's. He was a serious thorn in their flesh, even publicly calling them gangsters and a crooked, invisible government more than once in open session in Congress. He said in a speech in the House of Representatives in 1932:

"Mr. Chairman, we have in this country one of the most corrupt institutions the world has ever known. I refer to the Federal Reserve Board and the Federal Reserve Banks, Some people think that the Federal Reserve Bank is a United States Government institution. They are private monopolies which prey upon the people of these United States for the benefit of themselves and their foreign customers; foreign and domestic speculators and swindlers; and rich and predatory money lenders. In that dark crew of financial pirates there are those who would cut a man's throat to get a dollar out of his pocket; there are those who send money into states to buy votes to control our legislatures; there are those who maintain International propaganda for the purpose of deceiving us into granting of new concessions which will permit them to cover up their past misdeeds and set again in motion their gigantic train of crime."

"He didn't pull any punches, did he?"

"No. McFadden was incredibly vociferous and persistent. He just wouldn't go away. Like a stubborn wasp, buzzing round their heads. The cabal were furious. As a result, he received many death-threats before he was finally fatally poisoned, after two previous failed assassination attempts. He was about to take legal action to impeach the leaders of the Federal Reserve before he was killed. The case was quietly dropped after his death.

President Woodrow Wilson said in *The New Freedom,*

"Since I entered politics, I have chiefly had men's views confided to me privately. Some of the biggest men in the United States, in the field of commerce and manufacture, are afraid of something. They know that there is a power somewhere so organized, so subtle, so watchful, so interlocked, so complete, so pervasive, that they had better not speak above their breath when they speak in condemnation of it."

Despite many warnings by honest, prominent men, Woodrow Wilson signed the 1913 Federal Reserve Act. Some sources say he was blackmailed into it, but there's no actual proof of this. Anyway, he later said he bitterly regretted it.

President Franklin D. Roosevelt was quoted in a book about his personal letters in 1933:

"The real truth of the matter is, as you and I know, that a financial element in the large centers has owned the government ever since the days of Andrew Jackson."

The controlled mainstream press, who are a vital arm of the conspiracy, usually just ignore the whistleblowers where they can. They want to keep control of the narrative for themselves.

Congressman Oscar Callaway said in 1917:

"In March, 1915, the J.P. Morgan interests, the steel, shipbuilding, and power interests, and their subsidiary organizations, got together 12 men high up in the newspaper world and employed them to select the most influential newspapers in the United States and sufficient number of them to control generally the policy of the daily press. They found it was only necessary to purchase the control of twenty-five of the greatest papers.

An agreement was reached; the policy of the papers was bought, to be paid for by the month; an editor was furnished for each paper to properly supervise and edit information regarding the questions of preparedness, militarism, financial policies, and other things of national and international nature considered vital to the interests of the purchasers."

Calum was listening avidly as Jonnie proceeded.

"There seem to be no limits to the cabal's attempts to use the CIA and the controlled Press to undermine free speech. In the 1950's the CIA, an integral and necessary part of the conspiracy, set up Operation Mockingbird to manipulate news media for propaganda purposes. This included recruiting leading American journalists to form a network to present the CIA and its policies in a favourable light. It funded various student societies and magazines as propaganda fronts. Later, it also expanded its operation to include a secret initiative to influence foreign media and political campaigns and illegally tapped the phones of journalists who were inimical to their objectives."

Johnnie sighed. "Nothing's changed. Indeed, it'll get much worse. Look, there _are_ some brave, honest, independent journalists. Of course, there are. What's more, there are others who deplore the situation but realise that, at present, they are spitting against the wind. So, they pick issues where they are able to fight for truth and fairness with less censorship and interference. Yes, this can be seen as a little cowardly, but they are still "pushing the envelope" as much as they can. Indeed, they would argue they are realists and if they persisted in the "wrong" areas, their voices would not be heard at all.

Free speech will start to be seriously eroded around the start of next century. In addition to the muzzling of the press, censorship will be nurtured within your own universities and colleges. Some extreme left-wing, pseudo-liberal professors and lecturers with their own agenda will dominate many campuses, encouraging their students to force proponents of opposing views who have been invited by non-Leftist students to speak at their debating societies to be banned from appearing. They will portray all non-leftists as extreme right-wing, evil fascists ("if you're not with us, you're against us" syndrome). This will be most prevalent in subjects related to the Humanities, teaching of which will effectively be destroyed as a serious intellectual exercise in such universities by the first few decades of next century.

Their cunning, disingenuous excuse for threatening free speech will be that the arguments of their opponents are so offensive to some disadvantaged people, they cause unacceptable distress, These views should, therefore, not be allowed to be voiced. Now, there are indeed many underprivileged people in the world, as these extreme leftists say, such as the severely disabled and the selfless people who care for them, people who are being oppressed all over the world, or suffering racial or religious prejudice, or people experiencing humiliation because they are struggling with their sexuality. However, for the extreme Left to hijack these feelings of alienation and pretend this is why they want free speech censored is insincere and dishonest.

The real truth is it's quite simply a duplicitous way of killing reasoned debate. It's quite right that oppressed people should be protected…….but not from rational, open debate. What's more, they play the man, not the ball. That way, they can ignore the actual issues. Attack and lie about your adversary's character to undermine their credibility. Use emotional language to cloud the facts, and paint all your opponents as uncivilized, rabid "fascists." This word "fascist" will soon become a catch-all for anyone the extreme left doesn't like. At all costs, they try to deflect debate about the actual issues, instead varnishing everything with virtue-signaling casuistry. In other words, they use coercion dressed up as niceness; despotism cloaked as altruism.

Politically, they describe themselves as liberals, but classical liberals like Gladstone, Asquith or Lloyd George wouldn't recognise these beliefs as remotely liberal. They're actually old-style Marxists. However, history shows that not one Marxist regime has ever succeeded, either financially or sociologically. It has led to tyrannical, inhuman, failed states who murdered tens of millions of their own citizens. States that can only stop mass defection of their population to non-Marxist countries by forcing their citizens to stay by violent coercion, creating an Orwellian prison. How catastrophic is this to the credibility of a political belief system?

So, if you're devious and still want to promote an ideology that have been discredited by history, what do you do? Well...... you come up with a new philosophy where evidence is not important. Pronounce that evidence is subjective. That no belief is more right or wrong than any other. That all opinions have equal validity. A kind of relativistic mumbo-jumbo which says there is no objective truth, reality, reason or morality. Bingo! You've just invented Postmodernism. How clever. Most of these crypto-Marxists are Postmodernists.

They also add an attractive gloss to it, dressing it up as something nice and cuddly, looking after the interests of the ordinary man, especially the oppressed.

To be fair, there are many of the leftists whose motives are genuinely altruistic and honourable. Being on the Left is a perfectly reasonable position, as long as you're not an extremist. However, even these genuine ones are not doing themselves any favours by preventing their beliefs being challenged. You can't live in a bunker all your life. At some stage, the world is bound to notice the Emperor isn't wearing any clothes.

New pseudo-subjects without proper academic rigour will be introduced to the curriculum in these universities. You'll easily spot them when they arrive on the scene. The aim of these courses is to promote the teachers' own sociological ideology. In practice, only students who already believe in the biased narrative behind these studies would go near these courses with a barge-pole. The syllabus itself is a red light, because it shows up what the agenda really is. However, if some "un-reconstructed" students somehow decide to join the course and express views opposed to the received dogma, they just give them low marks. If these insubordinate students still don't get the message and persist, they often create enmity against them amongst their fellow students. These "monoversities," where the extreme Left drives out dissent will spring up all over the place like a nasty virus.

The end-game will be for these illiberal autocrats to push for expression of their opponents' inconvenient views to be made a criminal offence. Even the words they use to describe their own views are Orwellian. Such as "progressive." Can you progress backwards, I wonder? As Orwell warned many years ago, "First they steal the words, then they steal the meaning."

"Don't some views sometimes cause genuine offence to other people, though?"

"Of course they do. Most views offend some-one but this is what debate is all about, a free exchange of views. If some subjects are taboo because those on one side are so mentally fragile they can't accept reasonable scrutiny of their opinions without a panic attack, or bursting into tears, or walking out, something is badly wrong. Also, where do you draw the line between acceptable and unacceptable views? Even more important is the "elephant in the room" question. Who decides? Now, who do you think would be given that job? The

Campaign for Plain English? I don't think so, somehow. Yes, I'm sure you've worked it out already. The Thought Police. Bravely stamping down on Wrongthink, Thoughtcrime won't be tolerated. This scorn for free speech will be accompanied by a huge decline in intellectual rigour and dumbing down of standards. No democracy can long survive a sustained two-pronged attack on free speech and intellectual standards. These two things are essential planks of a successful, fair and sane society."

Calum's illusions were disintegrating by the minute. It was a lot to absorb in a short space of time.

Chapter 10

Calum was obviously surprised and disappointed at the future Johnnie was painting but, on the other hand it was a fascinating challenge too and Calum liked a challenge.

Johnnie pressed on. "Getting back to the invisible government, John F. Hylan, New York City Mayor said in the New York Times on March 26, 1922 in a rare moment of open political reporting on this subject by that newspaper:

"The real menace of our Republic is the invisible government, which like a giant octopus sprawls its slimy legs over our cities, states and nation. The little coterie of powerful international bankers virtually run the United States government for their own selfish purposes. They practically control both parties and control the majority of the newspapers and magazines in this country. They use the columns of these papers to club into submission or drive out of office public officials who refuse to do the bidding of the powerful corrupt cliques which compose the invisible government. It operates under cover of a self-created screen and seizes our executive officers, legislative bodies, schools, courts, newspapers and every agency created for the public protection."

In 1987, Daniel Inouyi, the Senator for Hawaii will state in a filmed speech in the Senate in 1987, revealed:

"There exists a shadowy government with its own Air Force, its own Navy, its own fundraising mechanism, and the ability to pursue its own ideas of national interest, free from all checks and balances, and free from the law itself."

Calum raised his eyebrows and gaped in astonishment. "Johnnie, how on Earth can you remember all these speeches word for word?"

"Because my IQ and memory capacity are streets ahead of yours," he stated matter-of-factly without conceit. He continued.

"Kennedy said in a filmed speech last year:

"The very word "secrecy" is repugnant in a free and open society; and we are as a people inherently and historically opposed to secret societies, to secret oaths and secret proceedings. For, we are opposed around the world by a monolithic and ruthless conspiracy that relies on covert means for expanding its sphere of influence – on infiltration instead of invasion, on subversion instead of elections, on intimidation instead of free choice, on guerrillas by night instead of armies by day. It is a system which has conscripted vast human and material resources into the building of a tightly knit, highly efficient machine that combines military, diplomatic, intelligence, economic, scientific and political operations. Its preparations are concealed, not published. Its mistakes are buried not headlined. Its dissenters are silenced, not praised. No expenditure is questioned, no rumour is printed, no secret is revealed."

Some people have interpreted this speech as referring to communism, but the first sentence doesn't fit this interpretation at all."

"I've never seen anything about that speech on the telly."

Johnnie smiled wryly. "You're not likely to."

Narrowing his eyes, he offered Calum more advice. Surely, says the man in the street, something as evil as this would be all over the papers and TV? It's so shocking, surely it can't be hidden. The BBC, that bastion of truth, and fearless exposer of wrongdoers, would have done a documentary on it. Wrong. It's a no-go area for the BBC too. So, for now, keep your own counsel because if not, at first, you'll be marginalised as a crank and your reputation damaged."

"What's the cabal's main aim?"

"To set up what they call a New World Order. A worldwide police state monitored by constant surveillance of the population with complete control in their hands. I know that sounds way over the top, paranoid and fanciful, but it's true. The highly credible, prominent insiders I'm quoting are only a few of the scores of prominent people exposing the conspiracy. The tip of the iceberg. I could have given you ten times as many quotes, but we haven't got the time…..and I don't want to test your boredom threshold too much. However, let's put it this way. If I'm deluded, or exaggerating, then I'm in crowded and exalted company."

"Wow! This is scary stuff."

Leaning his arms on the table, Johnnie continued with a sombre and slightly sad expression. "The cover-up of the Kennedy conspiracy by the invisible government will be very efficient - and the consequences for many of the witnesses will be tragic. By the end of 1966, a total of eighteen material witnesses will have died. Six by gunfire, three in motor accidents, two by suspicious "suicides," one from a cut throat, one from a karate chop to the neck, three by heart attack and two by other natural causes. What do you reckon is the likelihood of this incidence of violent deaths happening by chance?

The famous and fearless investigative journalist, Dorothy Kilgallen, will be the only reporter to obtain a full private interview with Jack Ruby after he goes to jail for murdering Oswald. After this interview, she'll announce she is going to break the real story and have the biggest scoop of the century. She was going to write a book, she said, to blow the whole conspiracy apart. Soon after this, she'll be found dead, officially from alcohol and drug abuse, although she'd never had any problem whatsoever with either in the past. Her family will protest that she was murdered but it'll make no difference to the official verdict. Dorothy had put together a secret dossier of evidence, documents and interviews which she kept close to her all the time. It will never be found.

At least 38 witnesses who claimed that one or more shots came from the general direction of the grassy knoll were, selectively, not called to give evidence at the Warren Commission, as you know, set up by President Johnson very soon after the assassination. The authorities need to conceal that there was more than one gunman because that would mean it was by definition a conspiracy, which would necessitate a criminal investigation. It will take 13 years after Kennedy's death for public opinion to finally force an official government re-investigation after the whitewash and downright fraud of the Warren Commission. The United States House of Representatives Select Committee on Assassinations will meet in 1976-78 and announce their official conclusion the following year that it was probably a conspiracy. Many of the public will be unaware of this decision because many newspapers will either ignore it or put it on a minor page. Unlike the fraudulent Warren Commission decision which was plastered all over the newspapers. The Judiciary themselves also effectively ignored the second enquiry, because there was no re-opening of the case. Why not?

One of the arguments made by critics of the Kennedy conspiracy theory will be that if there was a cover-up, it would crack apart. Someone would have been bound to talk. What a joke. There has been, and will be, no end of people doing just that. Witnesses whose testimonies will be smothered; witnesses deliberately excluded from the Warren Commission; murdered reporter Dorothy Kilgallen; doctors at Parklands hospital who were warned to keep their mouths shut, but bravely didn't; Jack Ruby, who said in a short filmed conversation on his way to his appeal hearing that Lyndon Johnson and other very prominent people were behind it; Madeleine Brown, Johnson's long-time mistress, whose filmed interview will expose a huge conspiracy; the female witness Acquilla Clemons, who said she saw <u>two</u> men involved in the killing of Officer Tippet and neither looked anything like Oswald, yet whose testimony was not given at the Warren Commission; the deaf and dumb man who saw someone fire a shot from behind the picket fence on the grassy knoll but was told to go home and forget about it when he went to report this at the FBI offices in Dallas; two strippers at Jack Ruby's "Carousel Club" who disclosed that Oswald and Ruby were close friends and who died violent deaths soon after; and the multitude of other witnesses who speak up but are not heard or die violent deaths because they know too much.

You could also include the people at the FBI who will be forced to admit the truth. That the Zapruder tape was edited and altered by the FBI with bungling inefficiency. More like deliberate fraud. Two frames of the film were missing, a splice was visible in two others, two were switched, and frame 284 was a repeat of the previous one. J. Edgar Hoover, Director of the FBI, will officially explain that the two switched frames were due to a printing error. "Life" Magazine, who had originally bought the tape from Zapruder, later officially announced that another four frames had been accidentally destroyed, and the adjacent frames damaged, by one of their photo lab technicians. Three further frames were also damaged and spliced out."

"Why did they need to edit it, anyway?" asked Calum.

"For two reasons. Firstly, to edit out the frames showing that very shortly after the first shot, Kennedy's driver, William Greer, deliberately stopped the car for many seconds to give the shooters an easier target and only drove away at speed when Kennedy's head exploded due to the final head-shot. Secondly and more importantly, they wanted to make the fatal head-shot look like it came from the rear, not from the right-front. However, hard as they tried, this proved an impossibility, which is why the public were never shown the movie film on network television for 12 years. The outrage that followed this delayed showing led eventually to the 1976-78 Senate re-investigation. The public were shocked that the description of events given by the Warren Commission bore little resemblance to what the film revealed - even after it had been "doctored.""

"Why did they need to kill JFK in the first place?"

"Lots of reasons. He was coming up with radical policies they couldn't live with. For example, he wanted good relations and peace with the Soviet Union, he was looking to pull out of the Vietnam

War and he threatened to "smash the CIA into a thousand pieces" because he had seen they were out of control during the "Bay of Pigs" fiasco. He and his brother, Robert, as Attorney General had so severely disrupted the plans of so many powerful, crooked interest-groups, they were practically queuing up to kill him. He also knew what the cabal's aims were and was determined to frustrate them. However, his worst crime from the cabal's point of view was to start printing and issuing currency directly through the Treasury, cutting out the Federal Reserve. If this continued, the cabal would lose its huge, primary source of income. Without the Fed's ability to control the economy and the massive money they make from creating currency, the cabal would soon be fatally holed below the waterline. Kennedy had to go,,,,,,,,and soon.

After Lyndon Johnson, who was an integral part of the Kennedy assassination conspiracy, succeeded Kennedy, he quietly stopped the issue of notes through the Treasury and withdrew the ones Kennedy had already issued. Also, far from pulling out of Vietnam, he escalated the war. He was the cabal's man in the White House. If you read biographies of Johnson after his death, they will show he was a mendacious crook who had fixed Senate elections and arranged for the murders of people who got in his way. Barr McClennan, an attorney who worked for the law firm who acted for Johnson for many years, will say in about forty years time that Johnson was part of the plot to kill JFK."

Johnnie held up four fingers. "Four American presidents have been assassinated - Lincoln, Garfield, McKinlay and Kennedy. They had one significant thing in common. They had all just reversed the existing monetary policy by starting to issue currency directly through the Treasury, by-passing the central bankers. Or announced they were going to. Abe Lincoln, for example, refused to borrow from the central bankers at usurous interest rates to fund the cost of the Civil War against the Confederacy and issued "greenbacks" through the Treasury instead. In each case, the murdered president's successors reversed the policy. Is all this a coincidence? It could very well be. It's certainly not an open and shut case, but I think it's very suspicious.

The wily German Chancellor, Otto von Bismarck, principal creator of the modern German state, was one of the cleverest men in history. As a shrewd, hard-nosed, pragmatic, militaristic leader, he was not prone to flights of fancy. As the ultimate insider, he understood exactly what was going on in world politics. He said in 1865:

"The division of the United States into federations of equal force was decided long before the Civil War by the high financial powers of Europe. These bankers were afraid that the United States, if they remained in one block and as one nation, would attain economic and financial independence, which would upset their financial domination over the world. The voice of the Rothschilds prevailed. Therefore they sent their emissaries into the field to exploit the question of slavery and to open an abyss between the two sections of the Union."

Johnnie frowned. "Another piece of important advice. Always, always look <u>behind</u> what the mainstream media tell you. They are owned by a small group of rich and devious men, part of the cabal, who only report the news truthfully on trivial, mundane things when it doesn't affect their secret agenda. However, as I've said, on matters of state, war and politics, the news is deliberately manipulated. As George Orwell predicted it would be, adding that in an age of universal deceit, telling the truth is a revolutionary act. His book "1984," written in 1948, will be an uncannily accurate predictive blueprint of the way the world will develop. Police states, control of the media, fuelling of hatred in the populace towards bogus or supposed enemies, constant warfare to benefit arms makers and the elite militarists and totally invasive surveillance of what everyone is doing or saying,. Close surveillance of the population is increasing exponentially. The plan's already well in motion."

He gathered his thoughts. "It's not true to say that Big Brother is coming. He's here already. Peter Hitchens, one of the honest, iconoclastic journalists of the next century, will comment when illegal government surveillance has become universally pernicious:

"We're always being told we're creating Britain's FBI. We're not. We're creating Britain's KGB."

"Surely it's only criminals that need to worry about surveillance, Johnnie? Honest people have nothing to fear."

"It depends entirely on the motives of those doing the surveillance. Since only a tyrannical regime would want, or need, such a widespread, invasive system, the question of motivation is fairly cut and dried."

Johnnie sat forward in his chair.

"Arguing that you don't care about the right to privacy because you have nothing to hide is no different from saying you don't care about free speech because you have nothing to say."

"True."

Johnnie continued his discourse. "Strangely, in one way, people living in Russia and other autocratic countries have an advantage. In the West, people swallow all the news whole, naively believing the mainstream newspapers and television wouldn't lie on big issues. They believe the Press is free and untrammelled. On the other hand, the Russians <u>know</u> what their newspapers and television tell them is lies. They don't believe a word of it. They know that, tragically, the truth behind world events is clouded, collusive and malign." He smiled ironically. "That's why you're not allowed to know it."

Calum listened closely, still enthralled and shocked, as Johnnie proceeded.

"Wars are hatched behind the scenes by superficially respectable men in dark blue suits with hidden, selfish motives. The international bankers have financed both sides in every major war for the last two hundred years…….. including both world wars. You don't believe this? Calum, it's not speculation. It's a matter of record.

In the First World War, the German Rothschild family financed Germany, the British Rothschilds financed Britain and the French Rothschilds financed France."

"What about the Second World War? Surely they didn't finance the Nazis as well?"

"Of course they did. The financiers don't care a jot. German multi-national giant 1.G. Farben, Union Bank of New York, and the Rockefellers via Standard Oil were particularly involved with financing the Nazis together with the Rothschilds and other US and European financiers. Whichever side wins a war, the financiers are always on the winning side. It's a bit like backing every horse in the Grand National and winning on all of them. The arms dealers also make billions selling weapons. What's more, they all did nothing to help the poor, beleaguered Jews caught up in the Holocaust, even though they were well aware what was going on. Why rock the boat?

Did you know that they even financed the Russian Revolution? Jacob Schiff, boss of Kuhn, Loeb & Company, the New York investment group and one of the Rothschild Brothers' agents in America, was one of the main financial backers. To begin with, he helped get both Lenin and Trotsky, who were in political exile, to Russia from Switzerland and USA respectively without being apprehended. Indeed, he worked with the German government to arrange for Lenin to travel in a sealed train all the way to Russia. Schiff also financed Japan in the Russo-Japanese War of 1904-05.

The bankers desperately wanted the Communists to succeed in deposing the Tsar, one of their bêtes noires, who wasn't dependent on them and had been hostile to the cabal's interests all along. A mass meeting was held at Carnegie Hall On March 23, 1917 to celebrate the end of tsarist rule. The following day, the New York Times published a telegram from Jacob Schiff, which had been sent to the meeting to be read out to the assembly of socialists in the meeting. He expressed his apologies that he could not be there, then went on to express his pleasure at the success of the revolution, saying "it's what we had hoped and striven for these long years."

The Bolshevik leaders were easier to control and they stayed on very friendly terms with them well after the revolution. The other principal reasons for the bankers' support were to get control of the Russian oilfields and other industrial concessions and to set up a Russian national central bank owned by them.

With the Tsar, who had opposed a foreign banker-owned state bank, out of the way, they had no problem getting these concessions from a grateful Lenin. The cabal obviously prefer Fascism and Communism to democracy. They're both autocratic and tyrannical systems and fit their own despotic aim of a world government, all-encompassing and run by them with a rod of iron. Unacceptable, radical views can be squashed and rebels removed from the scene. As Stalin said, "Ideas are more powerful than guns. We wouldn't let our enemies have guns, so why would we let them have ideas?"

They can still subvert democracies but they're too messy for comfort. Unpredictable. Too complex and multi-faceted to control absolutely. Henry Ford Senior understood what was going on:

"It is well enough that people do not understand our banking and monetary system, for if they did, I believe there would be a revolution before tomorrow morning." Ford said on another occasion, "The one aim of these financiers is world control by the creation of inextinguishable debts."

As Nathan Rothschild of Rothschild's Bank notoriously said, "I care not what puppet is placed upon the throne of England to rule the empire on which the sun never sets. The man who controls Britain's money supply controls the British Empire and I control Britain's money supply." With such control in their hands, the other parts of the cabal can be financed. Most of the public know nothing about this criminal conspiracy thanks to the muzzle on the press. The bankers create booms and busts to fleece the public and suit their plans. The Federal Reserve deliberately caused the economic crisis of 1929 and the subsequent depression."

He raised his index finger. "Calum, here's the sequence of events in the 1920's. Between 1923 and 1929, the Fed increased the money supply by an incredible 67% and made credit very easy to obtain, causing an economic boom. Shares rose fast and a huge number of the population feverishly bought shares seeing no end to the boom, which had been hyped in the controlled press. Many ordinary working class and middle class people bought shares on "margin," i.e. they only had to pay 10% of the price with the remainder being lent by financial institutions via the broker. In a rapidly rising market, the borrowers saw no problem with this. The sting in the tail, however, was that there was a "margin call" clause. This meant the loan could be called in at any time - payable within 24 hours. A few months before the collapse, the international financiers behind these loans gradually started to pull out surreptitiously from the market, selling their shares at high prices. Suddenly, on 24th October 1929, the lenders started to call in all the loans. As a result, millions of people and over 20,000 small banks outside the Federal Reserve system went bankrupt. Shares plummeted in value and were bought back very cheaply by the Fed bankers. They also bought the bankrupt companies and small banks for a pittance and repossessed personal property at knock-down prices."

Curtis Dall, President Franklin Roosevelt's son-in-law and a stockbroker at Lehman Brothers, stated in his autobiography,

"The depression was the calculated 'shearing' of the public by the World-Money powers, triggered by the planned sudden shortage of supply of call money in the New York money market. The One World Government leaders and their ever close bankers have now acquired full control of the money and credit machinery of the U.S. via the creation of the privately owned Federal Reserve Bank."

Calum was listening avidly. "I read somewhere that most of the international bankers are Jewish. Doesn't that reflect badly on Jews generally?"

"Yes, it does cause some ill-feeling against Jews among people who know what's going on. And in view of the bankers' appalling behaviour, that's not too surprising. However, this has to be looked at more intelligently and in context. These people are not bad because they're Jewish. They're bad because they're bad people. Similarly, good Jews are not good because they're Jewish. It's because they're good people. Like any group, Jews have their fair share of evil men. Would you tar <u>all</u> Christians with the mass-murders of the perpetrators of the Holocaust or the cruelties of the Crusaders? Of course not.

Throughout history, there have been countless brave and honourable Jews at the forefront in fighting against tyranny and injustice all over the world. There still are. When the cabal is eventually confronted, there will be many Jews amongst those fighting for freedom. Overall, Jewish contribution to human culture has been considerable – scientists, philosophers and many others. Also, most importantly, you mustn't forget that the vast majority of Jews are actually <u>victims</u> of the cabal, just as much as the rest of the population."

He paused. "No race or culture has a monopoly over good or evil."

Calum nodded in agreement.

Calum was reeling from an overdose of frightening information, (and mixed metaphors!), so Johnnie clasped his arm and smiled to raise his spirits.

"How will the cabal affect the confrontation between the West, Russia and China?"

"They'll be in the shadows, in the background, deliberately increasing the tension between countries by using false-flag events and saboteurs. They will deviously create hornets' nests and poke them, causing mayhem. The invisible government will create enmity between countries. They'll make the military confrontation more hateful and destructive when it comes. They'll push and manoeuvre for costly wars and they'll get them."

"Surely a world war will endanger them too. What's in it for them?"

"They'll be well shielded in their secret, protected places. The resulting world chaos will be the culmination of their whole psychopathic strategy. They believe that in the turmoil of global anarchy, they can step in as benevolent saviours and persuade the people to accept a one-world government, run by them, as the best way forward. This is the final pièce de resistance. It's the ultimate fulfilment of all their machinations. After the war, they will for a time succeed in these aims. Their control of the police and the army will be crucial. There's always a large number of people who will follow orders even if these orders are plainly cruel and tyrannical. Also, with enough guile and chicanery, people can be persuaded to believe in lies for some considerable time. Voltaire said that those who can make you believe absurdities can make you commit atrocities."

Seeing Calum's downcast expression, Johnny put his hand on his shoulder. "Don't despair. Nothing in this world is forever. The time will come when things will change. Arrogance is their Achilles heel. It will make them over-confident. As the ancient Greeks would have said, hubris will lead to nemesis. The initial revelation of the conspiracy will come when prominent people are no longer prepared to suppress the truth. When they're first told the truth, most people will refuse to believe it. They'll reject it because they cannot bear to see their illusions shattered. The paradigm shift is too great. Yet, uncannily, there always seems to be a critical point at which a light suddenly switches on and everyone works out the truth at almost the same time. A tipping point.

The take-over by the cabal won't last for many years. The people will organise and fight back. It won't be easy because the cabal will be in full control at the start. However, in the end, the army and police will eventually mutiny which will be the beginning of the end for the cabal. Until the tipping point, don't cross them. Let other brave men hasten the dawn. Your primary task is too important to risk you not being around to complete it." Johnnie looked at Calum reassuringly. "That's your destiny."

At the same time, of course, something immensely powerful is at work in the background all the time. Something primeval and ineffable. The slow, grinding of the mysterious 500-year wheel as it turns. The inscrutable, unrelenting march of history."

He gave Calum a consoling smile. It was tough for Calum to take in all this depressing information at one go. "For the rest of your life, I want you to think deeply about why the human race is here. You won't come up with a definitive solution because it's an impossible task. The ultimate, unanswerable $64,000 question. However, using your logic and humanity of spirit, form your own theory about what the likeliest answer is. This is not an arid, academic exercise. There are good reasons to do this. Firstly, you can create your own ethical basis for how you want to live your life and secondly, it will give you focus and clarify your mind. It won't be like the Laws of the Medes and the Persians. It will be a fluid hypothesis, not static, so it will gradually change a little as your life progresses. However, without this on-going vision of celestial, cosmic purpose you'll be rudderless and your focus on life will be nebulous and unfulfilling.

Here are a few basics to start you off. Be ashamed when you should be, but don't wallow in it. Be proud when you should be, but not for too long. Don't ever look down on people in a lower position in life. Some of the reasons they're there are not always within their control. Often, they were dealt a particularly awful hand at the start. There, but for the grace of God………..

Above all, be humane and forgiving. This is not a sign of weakness. It's a sign of spiritual strength. If the philosophy you've worked out doesn't include these two words, you need to tear up the script and start again. Even looking at it from a pragmatic point of view, let alone a moral one, if you refuse to forgive someone, you're the loser. The perpetrator just carries on with his life, unaffected, possibly laughing up his sleeve, while you get stressed chewing it over all the time. Spit it out. It's bad for you.

Another thing. Remember, a good indicator of a person's character is how he treats people who can't do him any good, and how he treats people who can't fight back. This profound sentiment was expressed by an American agony aunt, believe it or not! Also, be brave, otherwise you'll lose respect for yourself and the world desperately needs brave men and women. Finally, be optimistic and positive. Don't be gloomy. A gloomy man rarely prospers. And even if he does, he gets no pleasure from it. It's the sign of a dull, sickly, damaged spirit."

"This is essentially Christian philosophy, surely?"

"Yes, it is. Most religions are altruistic, so many of the precepts I've set out are common to all religions. "Treat others well and lead a virtuous life." However, in my opinion, and I stress in my opinion, the things Christ did and said during his time on Earth are the best blueprint for how to lead your life. There is also one fantastic thing that is unique to Christianity."

"What's that?"

"The belief that no matter what you've done wrong in your life, providing you <u>truly</u> repent, you will be forgiven. That's an incredibly gracious and powerful promise."

They both thought on this for a few moments. Johnnie expanded on his views. "It's been said, wisely, that certainty is the enemy of truth. Certainty is the error that has caused most of the atrocities committed by some religious people over the centuries. You know how it goes, it's always the same. "We <u>know</u> our beliefs are correct and therefore yours are beneath contempt. So we will try to persuade you to recant, by force if necessary." Conversely, true religious sages throughout history have been riven by doubt at times during their lives, because they're intelligent, truly spiritual and don't have closed minds. Indeed, if it ever did become an actual certainty, religion would become a science, not a religion!

For what it's worth, my own "take" on the Grand Purpose is unconventional in some ways. I believe Mankind are attending a unique school for their souls to learn and progress. You've been thrown suddenly from the warm bosom of some spiritually congenial place into a bear-pit, the day-to-day world. Deliberately and unceremoniously. Without being told why. However, it's for your own good, for your souls to grow spiritually. It's a spiritual test. You have to survive, to negotiate the bear-pit and cope with the new, unexpected rules of tooth and claw, look after your own safety and comfort, yet somehow manage to help as many people as possible along the way. <u>And</u>...........leave some positive legacy behind at the end."

"Not a difficult assignment really, is it?" laughed Calum.

Johnnie put his hands in the air, palms out. "I didn't make the rules. God's a tough schoolmaster all right but steel's not strong until it's been tempered by heat."

"What about reincarnation?"

"It makes complete sense to me. You come back again and again to try to resolve and make amends for what you did wrong previously. You also receive recompense in the next incarnation for what you did right - and what was wrongly done to you previously. Effectively, you reap what you sow. If you only live here once and there is no reincarnation and you die as a baby at two months old with a damaged brain, what's the fairness or significance of that life? What have you learnt? If, however, you return again and again, you have many chances for your spirit to grow and when that reaches a high point of development you move up on to the next level of existence. And over the years, there have been many cases of evidence to support reincarnation, albeit circumstantial.

The Christian Church, however, does not officially believe in it. Which is fair enough. No one knows for certain, after all. However, the reason for the rejection of reincarnation is partly political. At the time of Constantine, the first Christian Emperor, the Church had split into a few different sects with varying doctrines, like the Arians. Consequently, he realised that the official dogma had to be formalised and defined. So, he hosted a conference of top theologians, called the Council of Nicaea in 325AD to standardise the credo. They decided which precepts to retain and which to reject. The first became official doctrine, the others official heresy. From a practical, political standpoint, it was probably a necessary exercise. Reincarnation was accepted as a <u>fundamental</u> part of official dogma, However at a later religious council more than two centuries afterwards, it was declared heretical and it's remained so ever since."

Calum smiled broadly. "All this reminds me of the joke about the Eskimo and the local missionary priest. The Eskimo was confused and asked,

"If I didn't know about God and sin, would I go to hell?"

"No," said the priest, "not if you didn't know."

"Why on earth did you tell me, then?"

"Oh, by the way, Calum. Have you ever read Rudyard Kipling's poem "If"?"

Calum shook his head.

"Well, it's my favourite poem. It's very inspirational. If you're looking for some advice on how to live your life, you could do a lot worse than read it."

"How will you get home?"

"How I arrived." He smiled. "Via Callanish and the medallion device."

"Why Callanish?"

"It's a portal. There are many others in the world but this is the only one in the Western Isles." He smiled expansively. "It's an exhilarating way to travel and comparatively safe. We've recently invented time machines and trans-dimensional devices but travelling by machine is very dangerous on my planet at the present time. The technology is in the early stages and it's often lethal. We've got a temporary moratorium on using them after a series of tragic deaths. We're rushing to improve our technology all the time and in a few decades we should have cracked it."

"One last thing, Johnnie. I don't suppose you'll tell me how the stones work? It fascinates me." With a sad look, he added, "No doubt you'll tell me I wouldn't understand or I've no need to know."

Johnny rubbed his chin and thought for a few moments. "Go on then," he conceded. "Why not? Keep it to yourself, though. I'll keep it as simple as possible. When it's switched on, the medallion device creates a form of energy, very similar to lightning. A special kind of energy, which is not harmful at all to the human body. When I switch on the medallion, the amount of energy created is absolutely enormous. And it is quickly amplified in the atmosphere, resulting in a stream of anti-matter particles being generated.

Now, the internal crystalline make-up of these stones is quite unusual. So, their molecular structure is temporarily disrupted by these particles, causing the crystals to vibrate violently. Very rapidly, like a chain reaction, this effect increases exponentially. When it reaches a critical point, the natural vibrations within the body of anyone touching the stones change. They are then transported to another dimension – or plane, if you like. Every dimension has its own rate of vibration. It wouldn't be a different dimension if it didn't."

Calum clapped his hands. "That's great. Thanks, Johnnie. I think I understand it. Up to a point, anyway. Fascinating!"

Johnnie remembered something else. "I want to pass on this thought. President Theodore Roosevelt was, like most great men, including John F. Kennedy, deeply flawed as a human being. The proverbial feet of clay again. Nevertheless, he wrote this inspiring comment:

"It is not the critic who counts: not the man who points out how the strong man stumbles or where the doer of deeds could have done better. The credit belongs to the man who is actually in the arena, whose face is marred by dust and sweat and blood, who strives valiantly, who errs and comes up short again and again, because there is no effort without error or shortcoming, but who knows the great enthusiasms, the great devotions, who spends himself for a worthy cause; who, at the best, knows, in the end, the triumph of high achievement, and who, at the worst, if he fails, at least he fails while daring greatly, so that his place shall never be with those cold and timid souls who knew neither victory nor defeat."

Then Johnnie raised his hand. "I have one final, crucial thing to tell you. About fifteen years before the troubles start in earnest, you will receive a very short phone call. The caller will arrange to meet you. At that meeting, he will explain the time has come for you to start certain preparations. Follow his instructions to the letter."

Early next morning, they said their farewells with less emotion than Calum had expected. It had all been said the night before. With his rucksack on his back, Johnnie mounted his bike.

"Goodbye, Johnnie Quiet."

"Au revoir, Calum Sutcliffe."

About forty minutes later, a smartly dressed man in his early thirties with hard eyes and a business-like manner knocked on the door asking for Jan Larsen. On discovering Johnnie was no longer there, he showed a Ministry of Defence ID card and insisted on seeing his room. When he saw it had been cleared out, he pulled out a walkie-talkie and barked instructions into it. A few miles away, an

Air Force helicopter pilot answered the call and after some time flying around, he radio-ed back "I can see him. He's on a bike, just outside the village of Callanish. We'll pick him up."

Seeing the helicopter sweeping low towards him, Johnnie pedalled like a bat out of hell, climbing the small hill, following the road right towards the stones. The helicopter slowly descended and started to land about a hundred yards from the Grand Avenue. The pilot and his assistant both picked up their weapons as the craft landed. The persistent, frenzied cawing of a single crow seemed like a desperate sentinel warning Johnnie. To no avail. He was only about a minute's ride from safety, but he wouldn't make it in time. They would get to him first. How terribly sad. Such a waste.

However, suddenly something unexpected happened. Before the two soldiers could exit the helicopter, somewhere above the stones, there came a searing beam of white light. It struck the helicopter, which exploded in a bright orange ball of flames, killing its occupants. Johnnie was safe. The villagers heard the bang and found the wreckage. The "Stornoway Gazette" carried a lead story that week about an unfortunate helicopter crash. It got a one-paragraph entry in two of the national dailies and that was it. The MOD man and some of his colleagues called later in the day and despite Catriona's protests, went through the house with a fine tooth-comb. Without result. Calum overheard one of them say triumphantly, "We've got the "Loch Seaforth" and the airport covered. He can't swim the Minch, so we'll get him in the end." Calum thought not.

The following day, he found the note Johnnie had placed in his jacket pocket.

"Calum,

I know you're an avid reader of the Brahan Seer and even more so, Nostradamus. So, I've written some predictions in his general style as quatrains for you to decipher. It doesn't really matter if you get them or not. It's just something to remember me by, an intellectual riddle for you to enjoy solving:

**When two giants lose their rosy glow
A crescent beside the sickle rebels.
The lucky beast with a pearl in its claw
Offers aid and burns up the sickle.**

**The roses and star circle tremble, but are forced to engage.
Unnatural plagues and dusty winds of fire.
The king is paralysed but can't be captured.
By exhaustion, not by reason, Athena's bough prevails.**

Until another time,

Johnnie."

Epilogue

Dr. Calum Sutcliffe is now in his seventies but looks very much younger, slim, fit and incredibly healthy for his age. Thanks to Johnnie's compatriots, he should have a long time to live yet. He obtained a first class honours degree in medicine, then a masters degree in toxicology and a PhD in anthropology at Oxford. He is now a famous academic and taught at Oxford University for many years. He is currently doing medical research from his home in Callanish. His sister Kathy is a teacher of hard of hearing children in Inverness. Murdo died quite a few years ago but he did re-kindle his belief in an after-life, well before he passed away. However, he never lost his irreverent, iconoclastic sense of humour.

Many things have changed in Lewis too. Sunday is not as cheerless in Stornoway now. There are many places open, including some high-quality, contemporary restaurants. The Free Church still retains its own distinctive style of worship but the services are apparently much shorter now.

The ferry now comes from Ullapool, not Kyle of Lochalsh, cutting the journey by one and a half hours. Many mainlanders from Scotland and England have settled in the islands and the population is less homogeneous. Unfortunately, the Harris tweed business went into steep decline for over 40 years after its zenith in the 1960's, but it's now rising from the ashes to make a significant comeback with sharper, innovative marketing and targeting of new global markets. The Callanish Stones are now a "Historic Scotland" site with a visitor centre. Tourists flood in every day. Stornoway marags now have official Protected Geographical Status, like Cornish pasties and champagne. They're made by various butchers in Stornoway ....and the late Charlie Barley's family's Stornoway Black Pudding Company has expanded and sells its famous marags all over the world via the Internet.

Lewis has indeed moved with the times but, with any luck, the people will never lose their unique character and sense of humour. Slåinte mhath! (slantch-eh vah)

Calum often looks out over Loch Roag from the Grand Avenue with a wistful eye, wondering when the remarkable Johnnie Quiet will return. He was devastated by Johnnie's departure for some time. He'd been a second father to him. But in the end, he understood. He often re-reads the note Johnnie left him over sixty years ago. He has photocopied and re-photocopied it many times in case the original disintegrates. He has never shown the note to anyone…….but the framed words of Kipling's poem "If" have pride of place on his living room wall.

Calum was very excited yesterday. Out of the blue, he received a short, but very important, phone call.